McKenna's Mountain

The whip of the sweeping winds across the bleak Black Ridge Mountains could bury and smother life within minutes, but it couldn't hide the piercing screams echoing through the valleys. Tracking them down brought McKenna to the Dalton bound stage which he found ransacked, and with all the passengers brutally massacred. All, that is, but for one woman who led McKenna into an escapade he would never forget.

The mysterious woman orders McKenna, under threat of death, to guide her through the mountain ranges in search of a stolen hoard of gold. But they are not alone in this hunt – outlaws are equally desperate to get their hands on the loot. These men had killed in cold blood, and would kill again, and McKenna knew they were on his trail, tracking him silently, like shadow ghosts.

In this race against time, will McKenna find the hidden cache for his mysterious companion? Just who is she anyway? And will he escape with his own life intact?

By the same author

Rain Guns
Hennigan's Reach
Hennigan's Law
Shadow Hand
Bloodline
The Oldster
Border Kill
Bitter Sands
Go Hang the Man
Gun Loose
Drift Raiders
Trail Breaker
Shoot to Live
Plains' Wolf
Small-Town Gun

McKenna's Mountain

DAN CLAYMAKER

A Black Horse Western
ROBERT HALE · LONDON

© Dan Claymaker 2003
First published in Great Britain 2003

ISBN 0 7090 7307 0

Robert Hale Limited
Clerkenwell House
Clerkenwell Green
London EC1R 0HT

The right of Dan Claymaker to be identified as
author of this work has been asserted by him
in accordance with the Copyright, Design and
Patents Act 1988.

This one for P. B.

Typeset by
Derek Doyle & Associates, Liverpool.
Printed and bound in Great Britain by
Antony Rowe Limited, Wiltshire.

ONE

The whipping wind on that grey lifeless day swirled the dirt plain to a frenzy at the first drift of light, leaving nothing to see through the curtain of dust, nothing to feel save the cold, snapping bite, and no sounds to be heard above the high piercing whine – leastways not for a while.

And then he heard the scream.

It came muted and muffled like something torn from the ground, so that McKenna, hunched tight against his mount in the lean cover of the outcrop, had to strain to catch it. Another time, another place and he might have reckoned the sound for the call of a marsh bird, but this had been human and not too distant.

Somewhere out there to the North, he thought, squinting as he shielded his eyes against the gritty sting of the blow. But where, and who had made it? Maybe more to the point, why?

He rolled back against the rock, patted his mount, licked his lips and closed his eyes. Nothing he could do right now, anyhow. Might be an hour, nearer two, before the wind eased and the dust swirls settled. He had been caught in the Black Ridge Plains' blow before, many times, and had what he now rated a healthy respect for its unforgiving ferocity and downright meanness. You did not tangle lightly with a Black Ridge blow.

But somebody out there had and it had broken their nerve.

He opened his eyes on a tight squint and stared into what he could make out of the scudding clouds and fitful light. Be noon and beyond before the sun came through, but the threat of rain would pass on the wind and the plain stay as dry and parched as old bones.

He patted his mount again, eased his bandanna across his mouth and nose, and settled back to wait. And listen.

The light had lifted, white and brighter with the first of a pale sun, the wind eased to a low moan when McKenna stirred again at the outcrop, dusted himself down and spat the dirt from his mouth.

He waited a moment, still listening, then murmured quietly to the mount, rubbed its ears and led it into the teeth of the wind. He lowered his head to the swirling gusts, called his encouragement to the horse and crunched away through the dust and dirt towards the main trail heading north.

He would join it where he judged the person who had screamed might have been; somewhere close to the trail, in open country where the blow had nothing to break it, though he doubted he would find anything. Whoever had been out here must have moved on, forced to seek shelter however sparse.

Or been too exhausted and terrified to bother.

But why, he wondered, leaning into a stronger gust? Black Ridge was no place to be in bad weather, but he had yet to hear of it spooking a person to the point of screaming. And why only one scream? Had the person been silenced? Collapsed, passed out? Man or woman? More than one person; a wagon train, rough drifters? Not drifters, he decided. Drifters came and went like hunters and were not for screaming.

No, he pondered, trudging on, there had been only one person out here. Somebody on his or her own who had been driven to a point of terror and made only one sound before . . . before what?

The mount snorted and pulled back on the rein in McKenna's grip. 'Easy there, easy,' he soothed turning from a sudden whip of the wind. The mount backed again, its eyes suddenly wild, round and white as moons. 'Whoa . . . steady now,' murmured McKenna, shortening the rein as he closed on the horse's head and reached to run a hand over its nose. 'T'ain't the best of days, old gal, but, hell, you've seen 'em often enough. Recall the time when we—'

The mare snorted fiercely and put her full weight into dragging McKenna back. 'Whoa, whoa now. What's it about this place . . .' The blurred black shape loomed on the fitful light like a spreading stain as McKenna swung round to steady the mount. He tightened his grip on the shortened rein to hold the mare steady, wiped his eyes with his free hand and fixed his stance, his stare concentrated, his mind racing.

Unless the Black Ridge blow had fuddled his own

thinking, he was looking at what was left of last week's stage out of Wilmer for the border town of Dalton.

And even the wind could not clear the smell of death that drifted from it.

TWO

McKenna approached the abandoned stage slowly, carefully, picking his way on short, hesitant steps through the pieces of scattered luggage, the reluctant mare still snorting and tugging at the rein.

'Easy, easy,' he murmured against the whip of the wind, his gaze beginning to flit anxiously over the eerily static shapes as if he expected to hear them cry out.

He skirted an empty tin trunk, its contents long since blown to oblivion, a pair of tooled-leather boots, a mirror half-buried in the dirt, a hairbrush, smashed jewellery box, vanity case and, here and there, pinned to the stage by the wind like dead birds, the remnants of torn clothing.

McKenna hitched the mount to the spokes of a wheel, wiped the smears of dust from his eyes and continued to let his gaze wander over the chaos, the cold reality of what he knew he had yet to find growing in his mind. He swallowed, grunted and moved along the side of the stage to where a door had been ripped open to hang perilously on one hinge.

His eyes, already blurred and watering under the sting of the wind, narrowed to tight slits, as he peered into the stage, his nostrils twitching at the sight of the first dead body. A stoutish, middle-aged man, neatly if sombrely dressed, slumped in a corner seat, the blood-stain of a single shot to the heart darkening his frilled shirt like a cloud.

McKenna swallowed again and shifted his gaze. The head of the second dead body lay in the lap of the middle-aged man. A younger fellow here, McKenna judged, mid twenties or so; tailored buckskin jacket, broad-brimmed hat perched crazily on the back of his head, bone-handled Colt still holstered, a deck of cards spilled from his manicured fingers. A gambling man who had lived on his wits, a slick deal and a fast draw, but been too slow on this occasion to save his hide. The hole in his head was decisive enough.

McKenna's gaze shifted again to take in the third body – a preacher, man of the cloth, lean as a pole, sunken cheeks, grey staring eyes, slumped in the opposite corner, the Good Book still clutched in his hands, blood spots marking the cover.

McKenna's shoulders flexed on a sudden shudder as he turned from the grisly sight and levelled his gaze on the chaos, his thoughts lurching to the realization that a raider might still be here, waiting, watching, ready to add to the toll of the dead without blinking an eye. He grunted, took a hurried glance at the bodies, and moved on.

He found the bodies of the stage driver and the fellow who had ridden shotgun at a distance from the outfit. Both had been shot in the back, killed outright, he reckoned, as they had been ordered to scatter the horses. Whoever had planned and executed the raid had done so ruthlessly and with precision. No witnesses, no means of the stage moving on, nothing.

But who were the raiders, why had they hit the routine stage out of Wilmer, and where were they now?

McKenna's gaze examined the scattered luggage and personal belongings again. There was something chillingly systematic about the way they had been handled in spite of the chaos, as if every box, valise, bag, case, wallets even, had been searched with something specific in mind.

But what, he pondered, and who in these parts would go to such trouble, at the same time leaving any number of valuables to be simply lost?

This raid did not carry the mark of marauding Apache bucks with time on their hands who trailed the Black Ridge occasionally on their long trek to the northern hunting grounds. They would have taken everything of trade value.

Could the stage have been hit by scavenging gunslingers drifting through the territory? It was a possibility, thought McKenna. But drifters, however desperate, would not have risked leaving so many dead bodies, knowing that the line company would almost certainly launch a federal-backed search for the stage the minute it failed to show at Dalton. Drifters would have taken what they wanted or could sell and high-tailed it into the hills.

No, he decided, this raid had been carefully planned, even down to this remote spot on the plain where there was nothing to disturb. And that, he thought, turning his back on another swirling gust of wind, told him clear enough that the raiders had not hit just any stage. It had had to be this run with at least one particular passenger aboard. Which one, and why?

But since when had the stage for Dalton left on a scheduled run with only three passengers? It had always been company policy for the outfit to leave Wilmer with four paid-up travellers making the journey.

So where was the body of the fourth?

The mare snorted and stamped at the dirt as if to attract McKenna's attention.

'I hear yuh, old gal,' he murmured, leaning to the wind. 'Time we moved on. Make it fast to Dalton. Report what we've found here.' He pulled irritably at his flapping bandanna. 'Nothin' we can do, and that's for sure. Poor devils.'

He had reached the mare, laid a hand on her nose, his gaze still searching through the chaos for the dark shape of a fourth body, when the snapping click of a Colt hammer at his back rooted him to where he stood.

He swallowed slowly, but made no attempt to turn, his senses primed to every sound, the slightest movement.

'You got the edge on me there, mister,' he drawled. 'Matter of fact, I was just pullin' out, makin' for them hills up there,' he added almost lightly as his body tensed, his eyes working anxiously from the mount's nervous glare to the scatterings of the raid, the still-lifting swirls of dirt.

What chance of making a move, he wondered? A

quick lunge to the left, maybe managing to put the hanging door of the stage between himself and the gunman? Would there be the chance of reaching for his own piece? No saying who was standing at his back. One of the raiders? But, hell, why had this one stayed behind?

'Don't move! Raise your arms – slowly.'

McKenna stiffened at the clipped order. Goddamn it, the last thing he had expected – a woman's voice!

His arms moved, the right hand clearing his holstered Colt as he turned carefully, boots scuffing at the dirt, wind whipping his shirt and bandanna, the mare's breath hot on his back.

He peered hard into the pale, fitful light and the shape that seemed to shimmer on it.

'Unbuckle that gunbelt, mister, and step aside. No messing. This is not the time,' ordered the woman brusquely.

'Say that again, ma'am,' said McKenna, easing the belt to the ground. 'In fact, judgin' by what I seen here—'

'I have no interest in your judgements,' snapped the woman. 'All I want is your horse and you dead. And I'm in a hurry.'

THREE

Medium build, attractive behind the mask of smudged dirt and tear-stains; dark hair, wide eyes bright with a mixture of fear and fire; a neat figure, he guessed, beneath a once stylish but now ragged dress. She held the Colt in both hands, her arms at full stretch, the wind whipping round her, the dust continuing to swirl in hazy clouds.

'I ain't in no position to argue right now, ma'am,' said McKenna, his gaze fixed on the barrel of the Colt, 'but if you're one of the survivors of the massacre here, I'd sure like to help you.' He licked his gritty lips slowly. 'Seems to me there's been enough blood spilled.'

'You one of the raiders?' snapped the woman again. 'They send you back to check we're all dead?'

'No, ma'am, I ain't no raider. Do I look like one? Name's McKenna. Been trailin' hereabouts between Wilmer, the mountains and Dalton these past dozen years. Me and the mare here happen across the Black Ridge plain Spring and Fall. On our way to spend the summer up north. Got caught, as you can see, in the blow. It's a seasonal thing.' McKenna paused a moment, his gaze shifting quickly to the woman's face. 'And yourself, ma'am?'

The woman tossed strands of hair from her cheeks, her hands and arms tightening on a new aim.

'Don't get glib, mister,' she hissed, her lips thinning cynically. 'I haven't any good reason to believe what you say, or to trust you.'

'That's true enough, ma'am, you ain't. And reckonin' on what you've been through here, I'd feel the same. You care to tell me about it?'

'I don't see why I should, and like I said I'm in a hurry.'

McKenna's raised arms shifted a fraction. 'Way I see it, ma'am, we can't stand here all day in this weather, so you're either goin' to have to shoot me, or let me ease my arms a mite. What's it to be? I ain't got no hidden gun, no knife, and for what it's worth I ain't for killin' women. You got my word on it.'

'You may relax your arms,' said the woman after waiting a moment. 'But don't move none. I've still got you covered.' She gestured menacingly with the Colt.

'That much I can see, ma'am,' nodded McKenna, easing his arms to his sides as the wind whipped at his loose bandanna. 'You goin' to tell me what happened here?' he asked.

The woman tossed the hair from her cheeks again and bit nervously at her bottom lip. Her stare was unblinking.

'My name is Pendrick,' she murmured. 'Victoria Pendrick. That's my husband back there in the stage, the oldest of the three men, Charles Pendrick. The others are Jack Cutchean and the Reverend Dale. They were all shot. Point blank. Murdered. The driver and his partner along of them.' She swallowed quickly. 'I got lucky. I just ran blind into nowhere the minute the raiders attacked. Dropped behind an outcrop out there and didn't move again till the shooting was over and the men rode out.'

'I heard your scream,' said McKenna as he watched the levelled Colt begin to shift in the woman's grip.

'Nobody came to look for me,' the woman continued, her stare glazing. 'The raiders just murdered in cold blood. There was no sense to it. . . .' Her voice trailed away, she lowered the Colt and gazed vacantly into space, the wind teasing her dishevelled hair. 'It was madness.'

'They were lookin' for somethin' specific,' said McKenna. 'What happened here wasn't the work of hot-blooded Apaches, and even the worst of drifters wouldn't have left so much of value behind.' His gaze narrowed. 'These fellas knew what they were lookin' for. Any idea what?'

The woman jolted from her thoughts with a twitch of the Colt, a blink and a gaze that steadied on McKenna's face. 'Oh, yes, I know. But they didn't get it,' she grinned.

McKenna eased a slow step forward, his eyes flicking between the Colt and the woman's smudged grey face. 'What didn't they get?'

The Colt twitched again and the woman stiffened. 'You don't need to know,' she said icily. 'It isn't your business.'

'It's sure as hell goin' to be my business, ma'am, if them raiders come back in search of you and I'm stranded here without a horse! But I guess you'd reckon on that bein' none of *your* business.' McKenna spat dirt from his parched mouth. 'You know any of them raiders?'

'I might,' said the woman with a toss of her hair. 'Fact is, though, they're almost certain to be back – and before very long.'

'Well, don't let me hold you up, ma'am,' gestured McKenna cynically. 'You're totin' the gun there and you seem to be callin' the shots.' He spat again. 'But let me just warn you – in case you ain't had the time to notice – this blow ain't through yet, and unless you know the trail for Dalton—'

'Who said anything about Dalton?' clipped the woman. 'What makes you think I want to go to Dalton?'

McKenna swallowed and squinted against a whip of the wind. 'That's where this stage was headed, ma'am,' he said carefully. 'That's also where the law is. And you need the law, ma'am. Damn it, there's been five people killed here, deliberately, in cold blood and for nothin' – includin' your husband. That's the law's business by my reckonin'.'

The woman lowered the Colt and stared hard into McKenna's eyes. 'There's a range of mountains, the Scatterings, close by. Could we make it into them, Mr McKenna?'

McKenna frowned, wiped the drifting dirt from his face and was a full half-minute before he spoke again.

'I don't think I'm readin' you right, ma'am,' he croaked against another whip of the wind. 'Are you sayin' you don't want to go to Dalton to report this to the law; that you're goin' to leave the evidence of the

17

raid and the dead bodies to be found by the stageline when their men get to searchin' for the missin' outfit, while you, ma'am, high-tail it into the mountains?' He tightened his gaze. 'And why do that? Why ride into the Scatterings? They ain't a deal to offer, believe me. You plannin' on hidin' or somethin'?'

'I have business there,' said the woman flatly.

'Business? I ain't never heard of anybody doin' *business* in the Scatterings. There ain't nobody there to do business with, f'cris'sake – and beggin' your pardon. About all the Scatterings have got to offer—'

'We have one horse between us, Mr McKenna, and some distance to cover in a short space of time. Is the horse up to it? Can we make it?'

'Supposin' I have no wish to head into the mountains,' said McKenna, watchfully.

'Then I shall do the only thing I can do: take the horse, anyway, and leave you here; dead or alive is for you to decide.'

McKenna's eyes narrowed. 'And you probably would too,' he murmured.

'No probably about it,' clipped the woman, snapping the Colt back to a levelled aim. 'So what's it to be? You look to me to be a man who knows something of this territory, and that is precisely what I need right now. Your decision, Mr McKenna.' She squinted quickly into the strengthening sunlight through the dust clouds. 'Soon as it's calmed some, the raiders will be back. Best state your intentions. And quick about it!'

'No choice,' said McKenna, shrugging as he spread his arms. 'I'll get you into the Scatterings, ma'am, but only because I ain't for bein' around when them raiders return. But once we've made the mountains—'

'One thing at a time, Mr McKenna. Let's not plan too far ahead.'

McKenna grunted and looked round him. 'We'll help ourselves to the shotgun's Winchester. Might need it. Couple of extra blankets. Warm clothin' for yourself, ma'am. It can get a mite chilly up there in them rocks. Anythin' you rate of personal value, but keep it light. The old mare there ain't for heavy loads.' He bent carefully to pick up his gunbelt and holstered Colt. 'And then we ride,' he added with a simple nod to the north.

McKenna and Victoria Pendrick were exactly one hour clear of the scene of the raid and had the foothills of the Scatterings in their sight when six riders reached the abandoned stage, searched the area and, without dismounting, picked up the trail of the mare and followed north at speed and in silence.

They were already dressed and equipped for a stay in the mountains.

FOUR

The light had faded again on the scudding cloud cover and the shadows from the towering rock faces of the foothills thickened to a deeper black when McKenna finally reined the lathered mare to a halt, slid from the saddle and helped the woman to the ground.

'Horse has had about as much as she'll take for one day,' he said, patting the mare's neck. 'From here on in we walk.' He shielded his eyes against the flitting light as he scanned the surrounding peaks, then stared hard at Victoria. 'Might be an idea if you told me what precisely you have in mind, ma'am.' He grunted and shrugged his shoulders. 'Why are we here and not on the trail for Dalton, might be a starting point?'

Victoria adjusted the shawl across her shoulders and gazed carefully round the rocks and slopes to the lower reaches of the mountains.

'So these are the famous Scatterings,' she murmured as if to her thoughts. 'I seem to have known them all my life.'

'First time you've seen 'em?' asked McKenna.

'First time . . . but the late Mr Pendrick talked of

little else. The mountains were his life, and his ambition.'

'Ambition?' frowned McKenna.

'All his hopes for the future – our future as it was until. . . .' Virginia faltered a moment, brushed the hair from her cheeks, stiffened and pointed to the peaks. 'Somewhere up there, Mr McKenna, is a fortune in gold. My fortune. My gold.'

'Gold?' croaked McKenna as if the word had lodged in his throat. 'You say gold? Whose gold? Where did it come from, for God's sake? And how in hell did it get up there?' He slapped a flat hand on his thigh. 'I can tell you for a rock-solid, bone-dry fact, ma'am, that there ain't never been gold mined out of the Scatterings. Not ever. Not gold, not silver, not so much as—'

'This is illicit gold. Stolen years ago from the First Western Bank at North Canyon, and hidden. . . .'

The mare snorted violently, rolled her flanks and stamped a hoof on the hard rock track. McKenna took the reins in a short, tight grip, murmured to the mount and put a finger to his lips for Victoria to stay silent. 'Old lady's gettin' spooked some. That means we got company closin' fast,' he hissed. 'I'll climb higher; go take a look. You hold on here. Don't move.'

He handed the reins to the woman and slid away to the shadowed boulders on the nearby slopes.

The dust cloud was still at some distance, a cloak of grey and weak amber light swirling on the occasional gusts of the last of the blow and the pace of the shadowy riders.

McKenna reckoned on six men, moving fast, the dull

thud of hoofs and the jangle of hard-working tack echoing across the otherwise silent plain, the riders' destination on a direct line for the foothills of the mountains.

McKenna watched carefully for a moment, glanced quickly to left and right to take in the lie of the land, to the peaks to judge the onset of the twilight, then at the woman waiting below.

His thoughts drifted to a maze of the images: the massacre at the stage, Victoria Pendrick and her crazy account of a twenty-year-old bank raid and hidden gold. And now, damn it, a half-dozen riders crossing the Black Ridge at speed. Two spits to a barn door they were the stage raiders, and no odds, he reckoned, on who they were tracking.

He grunted, looked back at the plain and the dust cloud again, and eased clear of the boulders.

'You don't have to tell me,' said Victoria as McKenna rejoined her. 'I can guess: the raiders are out there.'

'And I wouldn't give a dollar bit to wager who they're chasin',' quipped McKenna. 'You say they didn't find what they wanted in the raid – so why are they hell-bent on findin' you, ma'am? What have you got that they want? And just where does illicit gold tie in with all this?'

He pulled the bandanna from his neck and wiped his face angrily. 'Them riders back there, whoever they are, wherever they've come from are hittin' the dirt at a pace. We might have a half-hour before we need to be higher and out of sight. But you, ma'am, have got just five minutes to do some fast explainin'. And I'm countin' right now.'

MCKENNA'S MOUNTAIN

*

Victoria Pendrick bit nervously at her lip, swished the hair into her neck and handed the reins to McKenna.

'I have this,' she began, reaching into her unbuttoned dress. 'It's a map given to me for safe-keeping by my husband. It pinpoints the exact location of the hidden gold. How Charles came by the document is a story too long to be told here.'

She handed the folded linen cloth to McKenna and buttoned her dress. 'The men heading this way are led by Frank Mattram who will stop at nothing – absolutely nothing as you've already witnessed – to get his hands on the map. I am equally determined he shan't.'

Victoria watched as McKenna wrapped the reins round his wrist and unfolded the map. 'Our intention,' she continued quietly, 'was for Charles, Jack Cutcheon and myself to reach Dalton, hire ourselves horses and supplies and trail into the mountains in search of the gold. It seems somebody was aware of our plans.' She stiffened. 'I am still resolved – probably more so now – to go ahead with the search. If it's a question—'

'You can't, you'd never make it,' said McKenna flatly, tracing a forefinger over the map. 'Not alone you wouldn't. If this map is anythin' like accurate, the gold is hidden somewhere up there among the high peaks, and trackin' into the Scatterings ain't no place for somebody who ain't familiar with 'em.' He raised his eyes. 'Specially not a woman on her own.'

'But you know the mountains, don't you, Mr McKenna? Would you consider—'

'No ma'am, I wouldn't, and I ain't sure as you should, seein' as how the gold – if it's still there – ain't rightly yours. It still belongs to the First Western Bank at North Canyon, don't it? It's their property. You should hand the map to the bank. Meantime. . . .'

The mare snorted, clipped a hoof on the rocks and rolled a flank into McKenna's back.

'Yeah,' grunted McKenna, 'meantime we still got bad company, and it's closin' fast.'

He handed the map to Victoria and unwound the reins from his wrist. 'Can't waste our time here, ma'am. Best be movin'. Somewhere higher.' He scanned the reaches beyond the foothills. 'If we can make it up there, to where them rocks stand clear of the line of brush, we can mebbe hole up 'til it's full dark.'

'And then?' asked Victoria.

'Make plans to get you to Dalton, ma'am, and eventually to North Canyon. Agreed?'

Victoria did not answer.

FIVE

McKenna's fingers spread like a spider's legs in their reach for the rifle, scrambled to a grip on the stock, then slowly, silently as if dragging a prey to a mouth, brought it to his side where he crouched in the cover of a rock mound.

He glanced quickly at the woman huddled a few feet away, at the mare hitched in the deepest of the gathering gloom, grunted to himself and went back to listening for the next trickling fall of pebbles.

It had taken less than an hour for the stage raiders to clear the plain and finally rein to a halt in the foothills. A taller, swarthy-faced, heavy-shouldered man – 'Frank Mattram', the woman had hissed – had set about directing the others, ordering them to fan out and scour the slopes to the last of the brush.

Now, with Mattram holed up in the rock cover to the left and his five sidekicks working and searching systematically higher, McKenna was beginning to sweat.

At least one of the men was close. The fall of pebbles had given him away. But how close and was he aware of McKenna and the woman? Had he smelled the horse, heard something, or had he simply sensed a presence?

Victoria stirred, snuggling into the scant warmth of the shawl, flattening the torn folds of her long dress across her knees and legs. She shivered, blinked on the deepening gloom and stared at McKenna, whose concentration on the slope to the brush was as tight as the rocks, the Winchester firm in his hand.

How long were they going to sit this out, she wondered? Would McKenna wait for full dark, make another move by night, perhaps look to saving his own skin and risk a break for Dalton? He had the opportunity even now, before Mattram and his men got closer.

She had stifled a shudder and half turned to attract McKenna's attention when the shadow loomed above her then swooped like a black hawk.

She gasped and fell back. McKenna spun round on the soles of his boots but too late to level the rifle as the man's body crashed across him.

McKenna choked and groaned on the impact, felt the man's breath hot on his face, heard the curse, the growl, then sprawled helpless under the first thudding blow.

He squirmed, braced his shoulders for the thrust against the pounding body above him, brought his knees under the attacker's thighs and heaved with all the strength he could summon.

The man grunted, growled, began to roll as McKenna struggled for a grip on the rifle.

'Sonofa-goddamn-bitch,' spat the raider under the force of McKenna's heave and smash of the rock-hard fist across his temple. He rolled aside, too dazed and confused now to be aware of McKenna settling a two-handed grip on the barrel of the Winchester, cleaving the weapon through a swishing arc above his head to bring the stock crashing over the man's skull.

The man's eyes widened for a moment, then rolled as his mouth opened on a groaning roar of curses and he lay still, blood oozing from the head wound.

'Take what you can from the horse and turn her loose,' spluttered McKenna, coming slowly to his knees, his gaze tight on the still shuddering woman. 'Do it!' he ordered. 'Now!'

'But how—' began Victoria.

'If I wasn't in this deep enough already, I'm sure as hell goin' to be up to my neck when Mattram and his boys get to this fella.' He took a deep breath and came to his feet. 'We're goin' to have to go higher,' he croaked, licking his lips, wincing at the already glowing bruise on his cheek. 'Nothin' else for it. But that ain't no place for the old mare there. She'll find her own way back to the trail. She'll know what to do.'

'I understand, but what—' tried Victoria again, tossing her hair across her shoulders.

'No time for debatin', ma'am. Just do as I say, and let's move before we get to givin' the buzzards a fresh meat supper!'

Victoria grabbed what she could from the mare, slapped her flank and urged her into the gloom.

The night had settled deep and silent when McKenna finally brought Victoria to new cover some seventy feet above the body of Mattram's gunslinger.

'Not high enough,' he said, helping her the last short distance to the widest part of the ledge fronting a maze of crevices and small caves. 'But this will do for now. I ain't reckonin' on Mattram makin' another move 'til sun-up. Then it might be a very different story.' He offered Victoria a blanket. 'Get what sleep you can, ma'am. Tomorrow could be hard goin'. And you'd best figure on gettin' out of that dress. You can't climb in an outfit like that. And there's goin' to be plenty of climbin'. You bet on it. Shirt and pants. Hope you packed 'em.'

Victoria nodded and patted the roll she had carried. 'And Dalton?' she asked. 'We still headin' there?'

'Don't see any reason to change,' said McKenna, unrolling his own blanket. 'But Mattram might have other ideas.' He eyed Victoria carefully. 'Want me to spell it out, ma'am? I will, anyhow.'

McKenna slung his blanket across his shoulder. 'I seem to have gotten myself in all this by chance. Could half wish your scream had got blown in another direction, but that weren't the case. Now, I'm neck deep in a stageline massacre, a woman with a map pin-pointin' the location of a hoard of stolen gold and, a whole sight more to the point, a handful of crazed, mean-minded gunslingers intent on gettin' their own bloodied hands on the map. I'm also trapped for the time bein' on a bleak mountainside, and it's very likely I've just put one of Mattram's gunslingers into a permanent sleep which the others ain't goin' to appreciate one bit. And I'd reckon for that puttin' a price on my head.'

He paused a moment to adjust the blanket and ease his weight to one hip. 'I'd say our lives ain't currently worth more than a handful of plain's dust, ma'am.'

Victoria stiffened and steadied her gaze on McKenna's face. 'I'm sorry for the problems I've caused you,' she said icily, 'but you're in no way obligated to me, Mr McKenna. Please feel entirely free to act as you think fit for your safety and leave whenever you're ready. Now if you wish.'

'Oh, no, ma'am,' quipped McKenna adjusting the blanket on his shoulder, 'I ain't for doin' that. I ain't desertin' you and I ain't leavin' this darned mountain without you. We're stickin' together, and we're goin' to Dalton – somehow.'

He turned to peer into the darkness of the drop to the foothills and, shadowed far beyond them in the pale moonlight, the Black Ridge plain where now the dirt and dust were still and silent and the wind no more than a whisper.

'It's the somehow that bothers me, ma'am,' he murmured.

Victoria slept fitfully in the shelter of a shallow cave. McKenna merely cat-napped between watching the woman and listening for some movement from Mattram and his men.

But it was not until an hour before the first crease of morning light in the eastern skies that he saw the slow, shadowy shapes begin to stir among the rocks and boulders below him.

He lay flat on the cold ledge and squinted to count, first Mattram then three of his sidekicks slip away to the twist of a narrow track. Four men moving, one man left to keep watch, one man out of action, perhaps permanently.

Trouble was, he thought, any path down to the foothills and the plain beyond would be impassable under the aim of the gunslinger posted to keep watch. Mattram, meanwhile, looked to be intent on moving higher by the less taxing route of the track. This would put him and his men above McKenna but out of gunshot range in less than an hour.

Time to move again, he decided.

He slid back to waken Victoria, urge her to silence and point to the smudged shapes of the crags and reaches high above them.

She had simply nodded, rolled her blanket, collected her pants and shirt and stepped into the darker recesses of a cave to change.

She checked that the map was safe in her shirt and left the dress where she dropped it.

SIX

They travelled light – the clothing they stood in, the rolled blankets, water canteens, strips of jerky, matches, two Colts, the Winchester, spare ammunition, knife and a length of rope.

'If it helps keep us movin' and alive,' McKenna had announced, 'it comes with us. Anythin' else is a waste. What I've seen of Mattram and his boys so far, they've come prepared for a stay up here.' He had paused a moment before adding: 'That would be on account of the gold, I take it?'

'Frank Mattram has only one thing on his mind at the moment,' Victoria had answered confidently, 'and I have it.' She had tapped the map in the folds of her shirt.

'Yeah, and I sure as hell wish you hadn't,' had been McKenna's muttered response.

They climbed in silence and without pausing for the next half-hour, McKenna slowing the pace only when he wished to establish the direction, listen for any sounds of Mattram and his men and watch for the shadows that were not supposed to shift save to the strengthening daylight.

He called a halt when they had reached the top of a ridge and slipped into the cover of a straggling outcrop of boulders.

'I'm holdin' to a steady line north for two reasons, ma'am, if you're interested. One, 'cus the goin's a mite easier, and two, twenty miles or so from here is where the main trail for Dalton skirts the western foothills of the Scatterings. We should make the trail in three days, trustin' to luck and avoidin' Mattram.'

'Twenty miles,' Victoria had murmured. 'That sounds some distance.'

'They'll be the longest twenty miles you'll ever travel, ma'am, take it from me. But if we stay steady and use our heads, we'll make seven miles a day, movin' as fast as the goin' permits through daylight, holin' up safe come nightfall. There's mountain creeks for fresh water, but there'll be no fires 'til it's necessary. I don't want Mattram closin' on us. We're mebbe ahead by a whisker right now, so let's keep it that way.'

McKenna turned to gaze over the drift from the ridge to a spread of rocky valley. 'We head down there, ma'am, huggin' the shade all the way, and no stoppin' 'til we reach that gulch far side of the valley. If Mattram's plannin' on another hit, this is where he'll do it from somewhere among those crags. You keep your head down, stay close, and keep movin'. Got it?'

'I think . . .' began Victoria, then dropped her bedroll where she stood. 'Perhaps there is another way. Maybe I should hand the map to Mattram. Just wait here till he reaches us and give it to him. It would be a lot easier.'

'Yes, ma'am, it would. And he would take it, I'm sure, and when he and his sidekicks had had their fill of you, he would cheerfully kill you, me right along of you. Right here in the mountains.' McKenna adjusted his hat. 'That's your other way; not one I'm prepared to take.'

'Why are you doing this, Mr McKenna? Why aren't you just looking to your own skin?'

'Oh, make no mistake, ma'am, I am. You bet! I'm as far on to the wrong side of Frank Mattram as you can get, and like you, I'm runnin' for my life up here. And the more we talk about it, the shorter that life could be gettin'. I don't give a damn about your map or any hidden gold, and I ain't fussed none as to who Mattram is or how he figures in all of this, but I sure as hell ain't leavin' them bodies out there on the plain to the buzzards without somebody bein' brought to book.'

McKenna tightened his gunbelt then took a grip on the rifle. 'And I ain't for havin' you harmed, whoever you are, for whatever crazed reason you're here. And that's a promise.' He turned to the drift to the valley. 'We're movin'. Don't forget your bedroll.'

The shadows thickened through the morning, shrouding half of the valley in a curtain of shade. 'Perfect,' McKenna had murmured to himself as he picked out the vague markings of a track and set the pace for the gulch.

Even so, he was conscious with every step he took of the eyes that might even now be watching from the higher ground, probing the shadow for the slightest movement, the merest glint of sunlight on a shifting surface. Mattram might be ruthless, but he was no hot-headed fool. He knew he had the advantage in numbers, strength and speed and perhaps had only to wait for the woman to weaken or the going to toughen for the map to be his.

What he did not know was anything of McKenna, save that he was a threat and had already put one of his men out of action, and could only speculate as to his involvement with Victoria Pendrick.

But Mattram's real dilemma, thought McKenna, lending a hand to Victoria to help her over a sprawl of boulders, was to know precisely what the woman planned. Was she intent on using the map and heading for wherever the gold was hidden, or was she escaping out of the Scatterings to wait on another opportunity of recovering the hoard? Did Mattram simply follow, let her lead him to the cache, or did he strike as soon as possible to secure the map?

Either way, he would still have to deal with McKenna.

Victoria slowed a moment to wipe the sweat from her neck and face. McKenna shielded his eyes against the burning glare and scanned the craggy surround. Nothing; no movements; nothing glinting; no sounds. Only the slow drift and lazy wheel of a circling buzzard.

'Gulch looks to be clear, ma'am,' he said, squinting ahead. 'We'll rest up there awhiles.'

'Anything of Mattram?' sighed Victoria tiredly.

'Nothin' so far, but he's out there somewhere. He ain't in no hurry yet.'

'But he will be.'

McKenna's gaze settled like the sun's glare on Victoria's stare. 'Yes, ma'am, I'm sure he will.' He shouldered the length of rope and settled the rifle. 'Meantime, we keep movin'.'

But they had taken no more than a half-dozen steps when the shot rang out, ricocheted through the rocks and whined to a haunting echo.

'Down, f'cris'sake! Down!' McKenna shouted the order on the back of the fading echo of the gunshot, at the same time pushing Victoria between the bulges of sprawling boulders.

A second shot spat, grazing the surface of a rock at McKenna's elbow. He reached out to press a hand across the woman's shoulders. 'Don't move,' he hissed. 'Not a muscle.'

He squinted into the glare to his left, his gaze scanning like a piercing beam across the crags, outcrops, reaches of shale and here and there the skeletal offerings of parched brush. It was a full minute and another shot before he caught the softest drift of smoke and then the flashing glint of a rifle barrel.

'Gotcha!' he grunted, licking at a surge of sweat.

'Is it Mattram?' croaked Victoria, laying her cheek on the boulder's face.

'More likely one of his sidekicks. But they ain't shootin' to kill. They could've done that two shots back.' McKenna's gaze tightened. 'This is a warnin'. Just givin' us due notice they're here and know precisely where we are.' He grunted again. 'Welcome!'

'So what do we do now?' squirmed Victoria, hunching her shoulders on the spreading lather of sweat at her back.

'They're goin' to pin us down for a time. Make us sweat it out through the blazin' heat. And every so often, the scumbag up there will fire off another warnin' shot, just close enough to keep us from movin'. They'll wait 'til the sun's moved round, then let us go. Old Apache trick, ma'am. Hell-fire exhaustin' for them without shade and forced to drink more water than they should.' He swallowed on his parched throat. 'So we don't drink a drop more than is necessary. Understood?'

'Is there nothing we can do, Mr McKenna?' frowned Victoria. 'I mean, couldn't we make a run for it, or something? Surely we don't just have to sit here like trapped animals, do we?' She brushed angrily at her damp, tangled hair.

'We do just that, ma'am. No choice. We take so much as a step out of these boulders, and I'm a dead man and you, Mrs Pendrick, are fodder for the boys.'

McKenna squinted into the rocky slopes of the valley again. 'Start countin' down the hours to them shadows movin' round,' he murmured. 'Then we move. And only then.'

SEVEN

The snake stirred as if from sleep, ranged its cold, wet gaze over the surfaces surrounding the rock, and slid silently into the shade as McKenna blinked and came fully awake.

He ran his tongue carefully over his cracked lips, tasted the salty sweat and reached for a water canteen. He unstoppered it and touched the woman lightly on the shoulder. 'Drink, ma'am,' he croaked, offering the canteen. 'We're about ready to move.'

Victoria shifted, drank swiftly, then wiped a hot, sticky hand over her burning face. 'Have they . . .' she began, losing the words on a gulp.

'Sun's goin' down, ma'am. Mattram's taken his men higher, above the gulch. He figures on us movin' there for the night. That's where he'll take us at first light t'morrow. We're goin' to disappoint him.'

'But I thought we were heading for the gulch.'

'We were, ma'am,' said McKenna, easing the cling of the shirt at his neck. 'Change of plan. We ain't walkin' into no trap. Mattram's been joined by the fella he left behind back there in the foothills. That makes five of the rats facin' us. Tough odds. So. . . .' He swigged gratefully from his own canteen. 'We'll move into the gulch, but only so deep. Mattram'll post only one lookout through the night, and that's when we'll be trailin' on, far as we can manage while it's dark.' He stoppered the canteen with a slap. 'You agree, ma'am?'

'But to where?' flustered Victoria. 'I mean, do you know the way? Will we be able to see anything?'

'I know the way, ma'am. You're goin' to have to trust me.'

'If there are now five men hunting us, don't you think it would be far more sensible to do as I've said – just hand over the map to Mattram? Let him get on with it?' Victoria ran the sticky hand over her face again. 'Wouldn't that still be the way out?

'Do as you please with the map, ma'am,' said McKenna. 'Leave it right there in the gulch where Mattram can find it, but it ain't goin' to make one spit of a difference. That sonofabitch is goin' to kill us anyhow. You don't think he's goin' to let us leave these mountains alive, do you? You're the only witness to the stage massacre. No, ma'am, Mattram's got his priorities, first things first: Kill us, then go for the gold.'

Victoria stifled a shudder in spite of the heat. 'So we go on?' she murmured.

'We go on,' said McKenna flatly as he turned to scan the steadily lengthening shadows.

A deepening shade had shrouded the boulders as the sun began to slip away in the west when McKenna gestured for Victoria to move and follow him.

They passed smoothly through the last of the stony

reaches to the gulch and were quickly into the still thicker shadows of sheer rock faces. McKenna's gaze had been concentrated more on the tracks ahead and those twisting into the half-lit crags than on the whereabouts of Mattram's men. He knew well enough where the look-out would be posted; knew too that he would be replaced every two hours by fresher, keener eyes.

The trick, he decided, was going to lie in being just that much sharper.

An hour had passed and the darkness settled when McKenna eventually signalled to Victoria for her to come closer. 'There's a rough track close by that'll take us higher,' he whispered as she squatted at his side. 'We're goin' to take it.'

'But how?' she hissed.

'We leave the blankets. Arrange some rocks beneath them; make it look as if there's bodies sleepin'. Might fool the look-out long enough to give us a start. Once up there – if we make it – we'll turn east. If memory serves me well there's a deeper valley, pretty remote, tucked between two of the highest peaks. That's where we need to be for now.' He squinted into the darkness. 'Let's just hope that scumbag look-out ain't got much of a taste for standin' guard.'

Twenty minutes later they had arranged the fake bodies beneath the blankets, collected their few other possessions and slid like shadowy snakes to the track.

It climbed at a gentle pace on a mixture of light sand and firm rocks for the first thirty feet, then narrowed and grew steeper, making the footholds harder to settle in the dark. McKenna led, holding wherever he could to the deepest shadows against the moonlight.

Victoria, conscious of the cold sweat across her back, the aching limbs, eyes that seemed too large and too round for their sockets, and the sheer effort of concentration, traced McKenna's steps as if she were the very shadow of him.

Her thoughts still swirled on the events since the massacre at the stage and the meeting with the drifting man who certainly knew the Scatterings but seemed to have no interest in the map to a fortune in gold. She smiled wryly to herself. She had yet to meet the man who could not be tempted by gold. . . .

'Easy there, ma'am,' urged McKenna on a tight urgent whisper. He nodded for her attention to focus above him.

Victoria squinted into the silhouetted shapes of rocks, ledges, jutting boulders. What was she looking for? A shape out of place, something McKenna had spotted. . . . And then she had it. A man, a look-out, seated half-turned to see into the gulch one way and, if he eased to his left, the faint, narrow line of the track to the other.

She swallowed, felt the sweat trickling down her spine, and gazed anxiously at McKenna. He gestured for silence and for her to stay exactly where she was, then slid the rope and water canteen from his shoulder, placed the knife between his teeth and climbed on soundlessly.

Victoria's blood ran like ice through her veins.

He felt gently for each handhold, relaxed his body to conserve his strength before hoisting himself to find the next safe surface for his feet. He breathed as easy as the effort allowed, moved as much by an instinct for the mountains as his careful judgement, his gaze tight on the man seated above him.

Hell, he thought, pausing for a moment, the fellow up there had only to shift his gaze a touch to the left, be disturbed by the slightest noise, the eerie bounce of a tumbling rock, and he could not fail to see. . . .

McKenna took a deep breath through flared nostrils, clenched his teeth on the blade of the knife and reached for the next hold, the first trickles of sweat oozing from his hat-band to his eyebrows.

Another few feet behind him; only a handful to go; one more hold, one more surface for his feet. . . . And still the look-out stayed concentrated on the gulch and the shapes beneath the blankets below him. Keep it that way, thought McKenna. Three minutes, maybe less if he could manage to heave himself to the next hold, stay steady, balanced, his energy building for the last effort that would bring him to the end of the track.

He eased gently, silently to his right, hopeful that the rocks would give him the grip he needed to come to the back of the man.

The look-out stirred, stifled a yawn, shifted the weight of the Winchester he nursed across his knees, flexed his arms, shrugged his shoulders.

The fellow was getting bored, restless, thought McKenna. One more heave.

He was out of the climb and on to a flatter surface in seconds, the knife tight in his right hand, the sweat gleaming on his face. The look-out, as if warned of a presence by some inner sense, half turned, both hands flat on the rifle, when McKenna made his lunge.

The blade went home, clean into the man's chest, on a sickening plunge and scrape against bone. The man's eyes widened, suddenly as round and white as pools dappled by moonlight, his mouth dropped open on a gurgling sigh, his arms and hands scrambled as if to a life of their own. He made to come upright, blood soaking his shirt, the Winchester sliding to the rocks, and toppled forward, into McKenna's waiting arms.

'Goddamn the sonofabitch,' groaned McKenna, easing the bulk to the side of a boulder. He replaced his hat with the man's, grabbed the rifle and slid breathlessly to the rock where the look-out had been seated.

'You stayin' awake up there, Charlie?' came a strained, hissing voice from the rocks deeper to McKenna's right.

McKenna stiffened, adjusted the hat and waved an arm.

'Relieve you in an hour,' came the voice again, and then fell silent.

McKenna blinked rapidly, swallowed deeply and wiped the sweat from his brow. 'Hell!' he murmured to himself before turning to peer along the track to where the woman waited, clinging to the rocks like a lizard.

He gestured for her to start climbing, aware for the first time of the sticky blood between his fingers.

EIGHT

'How long do we have?' gasped Victoria, struggling at McKenna's side down the moonlit stone and coarse brush slope.

'Nothin' like long enough, ma'am,' croaked McKenna, taking the woman's hand as she threatened to lose her balance in a skidding slide. 'Minute Mattram discovers the body of the look-out back there, all hell could break.' He came to a halt at the twisted stump of a dead tree and scanned the dark skies, the stars and the high yellow moon. 'Chances are he'll try surroundin' us, pinnin' us down 'til first light just like he planned at the gulch. He won't risk flyin' lead in the dark.'

Victoria shivered. 'Where are we heading? Do you know?'

'Well, ma'am,' said McKenna, settling his narrowed gaze on what he could make out of the surroundings, 'by my reckonin' we're at least two hours short of that valley I was tellin' you about. Shan't see that 'til sun-up. Country between here and where we're makin' for is pretty rough. Consolation bein' it's as bad for

Mattram as it is for us, so mebbe the odds even out some.' His gaze turned to the skies. 'Light's good – mebbe too good – so we keep movin' for now fast as we can.' He stared into Victoria's face. 'You goin' to make it?'

She stiffened, shook her sweat-greased hair into her neck and took a firm grip on the look-out's Winchester. 'I've come this far, Mr McKenna; survived the killings at the stage, climbed into these mountains, left behind a string of dead bodies. . . . Can it get any worse?'

'Oh, yes, ma'am,' said McKenna, 'it surely can – a whole sight worse.' He tightened the rope at his shoulder and swung the barrel of his own rifle to the other. 'But we ain't got the time for talkin' it through.'

Seconds later they had melted into the darkness like fading moonbeams.

McKenna's notion of 'pretty rough' going was not one shared easily by Victoria. The going, she quickly decided, was nothing short of a nightmare – never ending when there was so little to see and every stone, every chipping of loose rock became a life-threatening hazard.

She slithered, stumbled, lost her footing, her balance; was attacked, it seemed, by the clinging arms of dead brush, her shirt and pants ripped, exposed flesh cut, scraped and bruised. She was forced more than once to rely on McKenna's strength and patience to bring her back to her feet and wait the few vital seconds while she regained her breath, only to stumble on oblivious to time and direction.

No words were exchanged; the pained looks, the

anxious glances were enough when McKenna's gaze was not probing the darkness ahead, or assessing the chances of one of Mattram's men shadowing them.

They had moved quickly from the slope to a terrain of dips and lifts, ridges that fell away to shallow creeks, mounds that rose slowly, sometimes of sand and stone, sometimes of harsh bruising rock and the razor-edge fronds of parched brush.

But it was not until the moon had finally faded and the sky creased to the promise of first light, that McKenna drew Victoria into the shelter of an overhang at an outcrop, settled her on a boulder, uncorked her water canteen and offered it to her.

'Are we being followed?' she asked, leaning back, her eyes half-closed.

'You can bet to it,' grunted McKenna, 'but they ain't showin'. Not yet. Mebbe Mattram's still figurin' for us leadin' him to that gold.'

'Shall we?' asked Victoria bluntly, her eyes opening wide and bright. 'We could read the route from here – and we would stay alive.'

'Until Mattram had what he wanted, ma'am. And then he'd kill us.'

'You seem very certain about that.'

'I am very certain. There are no deals where gold's concerned, especially stolen gold. Never have been. This ain't no exception.' McKenna freshened his bandanna from his canteen. 'You'd have found that out for yourself soon enough, minute your husband. . . .' He fell silent, awkwardly conscious of where his thoughts had been heading. 'Sorry, ma'am, didn't mean to raise the matter.'

'No apology necessary, Mr McKenna.' Victoria looked

away to the shadows as if to examine her resolve. 'Charles Pendrick was not my husband,' she said quietly. 'What I told you back there at the stage was a lie.'

'But if he wasn't your husband—' began McKenna again.

'Pendrick won me in a game of high-stakes poker at the Five Stud Palace out at Bannenfield.' Victoria paused a moment, her gaze misting. 'I worked at the Palace, Mr McKenna. My real name is Victoria Foster and I was a bar girl, nothing more, nothing less. The Palace's owner wagered me against clearing the money he owed Pendrick. He lost. Pendrick got to own me. He insisted I marry him. I refused – for which I was duly punished.'

Victoria ripped open her shirt to reveal the scars criss-crossing the exposed firmness of her breasts. 'Pendrick's work,' she murmured on a chilled, icy voice. She took the folded map from the security of her girdle. 'But I got this,' she smiled. 'Now perhaps you can begin to understand. . . .'

The woman's voice faltered, cracked and was silenced on a long, deep swallow as her gaze turned with McKenna's to the shadow-streaked growing light and the crunching sound of approaching footfalls.

'One of Mattram's men?' murmured Victoria, her stare still wide and tight as she buttoned her shirt, half watching McKenna sidle to the edge of the over-hang's shade.

McKenna put a finger to his lips, crooked the Winchester in his right arm and settled lower, his gaze unblinking on the near impenetrable dawn gloom. The footfalls came on, feeling for every step, pausing, moving on, pausing again.

Victoria shivered on the sudden early day chill and the sense of her own fear. She reached for the second Winchester, drew it to her, came carefully to her feet and glanced quickly from McKenna to the shadows and back again to McKenna.

'Who is it?' she whispered. 'Can you see anything?'

McKenna's finger went back to his lips. He slid the rifle to a two-handed grip, came to his full height, adjusted the set of his hat to lower the brim a fraction, and stepped clear of the overhang.

He saw the shape of the approaching man as no more than a darker smudge of the grey light. He primed the Winchester with an exaggerated action, saw the shape halt, almost shimmer, then grow on the greyness as it turned full on to face him.

'Easy goes there, fella,' said McKenna. 'You got two choices here: you can either back off to wherever you came from and that'll be an end of it, or you can identify yourself and state your business.' McKenna spat across the dew-damp surface of a stone. 'What's it to be?'

'Go to hell!' growled a voice that grated like the rubbing of two rocks together. 'I ain't for listenin' to no two-bits, sonofabitch. . . .'

The man had taken two steps, a rifle ranged from waist level at his target, when McKenna's Winchester roared and blazed across the still, silent morning.

The man growled again, fired wild and high, stumbled forward. 'Where's that whorin' woman?' he choked. 'Where is she, damn you? And just who in the hell-of-tarnation are you?'

McKenna's rifle blazed again, this time burying its lead deep in the man's gut. 'You ain't never goin' to know, fella,' he muttered to himself as the Winchester roared its final shots and the man thudded face down in the rocks.

McKenna spun round, the Winchester still smoking in his grip, his eyes as dark as the last of the night. 'Get movin', f'cris'sake!' he snapped as Victoria left the overhang. 'The others ain't far behind and they won't be takin' kindly to the sight of another body!'

The blood on the rocks was still wet when Frank Mattram reached it.

NINE

The air was colder, thinner as McKenna and Victoria made their way at a pace from the overhang, climbing steadily towards the mist-shrouded peaks. 'Keep movin',' he had ordered, once clear of the body. 'Don't stop for nothin'. I ain't sure yet what Mattram will do. He might chase like the wind; he might stay patient. Let's hope for the patience.'

But his mind had fast filled with other images, faces and problems, particularly those surrounding the woman and the fate that had brought him to her path. She was not Victoria Pendrick; she had been a down-on-her-luck, badly treated bar girl, wagered like a handful of coins on a chance hand of cards. He had seen the unmistakable pain on her face when she had ripped open the shirt to reveal her scarred breasts.

Could he blame her for her animal-like possession and protection of the map? She saw the hidden gold as her freedom, the first opportunity in her life to shake off the two-bits, trail-stained men who had been her only payment to a roof over her head and the next square meal.

But there were still too many unanswered questions. How had Charles Pendrick come by the map in the first place? What was the tie between Pendrick and Cutcheon and where did Frank Mattram figure in all this?

And just why, damn it, had it been his unfortunate spin of the wheel to be out there on the Black Ridge plain when he had? Hell, he could have stayed holed-up in any one of a dozen places till the big blow had passed!

Fact was, though, he had been there; he had seen the grim leftovers of the massacre at the stage with his own eyes, and he had vowed to stay with the woman through the Scatterings to Dalton. But he had killed men, would kill again if he had to – damn it, he was fighting as much for his own life as the woman's – and Mattram was still there, still following, like any one of the wheeling buzzards up there, waiting for the chance to swoop.

That chance would come. It always did. It was in the nature of things.

Victoria stumbled, losing her grip on McKenna's hand. 'Are we clear yet?' she gasped, bent double now as she struggled to hold her balance.

McKenna took her arm and brought her closer. 'See them two peaks there?' he said, pointing ahead to the emerging sprawl of the mountains. 'Between them is where we're headin'. There's an old track – leastways, there was – that leads through and down to a valley. If we can make it that far, we might slip clear of Mattram.'

'He won't give up,' croaked Victoria, wiping the

sweat and dirt from her neck. 'He isn't the type, and he's waited too long.'

'You know him?' frowned McKenna.

'He drifted through Bannenfield from time to time; visited the Five Stud, but he was never ... in my company.' Victoria stared away for a moment. 'He got to know Pendrick and Jack Cutcheon, and that was the start. . . .' Her voice faded. 'Let's keep going, shall we?'

A dozen questions crowded in McKenna's mind, each one more demanding than the one before it, but the answers would have to wait, he decided. There was too much at stake right now.

He narrowed his gaze on the track they had taken from the overhang. No sign yet of anyone following; all quiet across a silent, empty landscape waiting on the full morning to break and the sun to climb above the peaks. Another two hours, and the rocks would be like hot coals to the touch, the air like something blown from the smithy's forge.

He grunted, broke his reverie and took Victoria's hand. 'Mattram's stayin' quiet for now. Like us, he's on foot. You can't risk horses this high on this terrain, so him and his boys ain't no better off and can't shift any faster than we can. Trouble is, o'course, he's lost three men to my reckonin', and that can't be sittin' too easy with him.'

'I'd say that's an understatement, Mr McKenna!' quipped Victoria. She had taken a step forward, when she hesitated and turned to stare at him. 'You've killed before, haven't you?' she said quietly.

McKenna gripped the Winchester and shrugged the rope aggressively across his shoulder. 'Trailin' this country ain't never been easy, ma'am, not even when there ain't the lure of gold to bend a man's mind. As for Mattram – well, ma'am, way I see it seems plain enough: Kill or be killed. Left his trade mark at the stage, didn't he? Don't take no reckonin'.' He narrowed his gaze on the peaks again. 'Mornin's comin' up fast. Let's make that valley before it gets too hot to fathom.'

There was a shimmering heat haze across the slopes of the drift to the valley when McKenna and Victoria left the last of the rocks, found the narrow dirt track between the towering twin peaks and passed into the welcoming shade of sheer rock faces.

'There it is, ma'am,' said McKenna almost cheerfully, 'the valley I spoke of. Plenty of brush and scrub, trees, and there's a creek on the far side where the water runs cool and fresh.'

'Somewhere to wash,' sighed Victoria, brushing aside a pestering fly. She smiled softly. 'An oasis, Mr McKenna. How on earth did you come to know of it?'

'That, ma'am, is a very long story and there ain't the time for the tellin' of it. We'll make the most of what we've got while we've got it – and that won't be long.' McKenna mopped his bandanna over his brow and cheeks. 'Might take Mattram a few hours to figure where we are, but he'll get to it eventually. What we've got to be sure of is that we use them hours to the best by keepin' ahead. If we can—'

'We're doing nothing until we've reached that creek, Mr McKenna, and I've relished that water! Please.'

McKenna adjusted the set of his hat and grunted. 'Guess you deserve that much, ma'am. But you're goin'' to have to make it fast. We must be movin' again before nightfall.'

'Then we'd best not waste another minute,' said Victoria, stepping away to the track and the prospect ahead.

In truth, and if he had cared to admit it, McKenna was no less grateful for the chance to rest up for an hour or so, take stock and try, best he could, to figure what Mattram's tactics would be from here on.

The scumbag was down to two sidekicks. Would he trust to them being all he needed to take the map, or had he developed a cautious respect for McKenna? Was he still gambling on Victoria leading him to the gold; would he sit back and wait; keep contact, but not show himself? For how long? And what precisely was at the back of the woman's mind?

He watched her with a careful eye as she moved quickly along the scrub-and-sand track to the creek. For all the effort of the trek, she was holding up well. She was strong, not shaken easily by the events around her, and still determined to survive and come out of this in one piece.

But survival for what, he wondered? She was here in the Scatterings with a map pin-pointing the whereabouts of a hoard of stolen gold. She might figure on being within reach of it. But would she give it up, forget it, against the greater need to reach Dalton alive? Or was she as bewitched by the prospect of gold as the men hunting her?

She did not have too long to show her hand.

The sun climbed high and fierce in a clear blue sky, the

silence settled like silk and the heat haze shimmered relentlessly through the mountain valley. Shade in the cover of sparse trees, boulders and rocks, was at a premium, but the area at the creek had offered the deepest and coolest.

Victoria had been quick to reach the flow where it tumbled over rocks and swirled to a calmer pool in the cover and shade of bulging boulders. She had disappeared from McKenna's view with an almost childike excitement at the promise of bathing.

McKenna had settled himself on the shaded side of the creek to check over the weapons and ammunition and keep the unwelcome company of his still-teeming thoughts and the questions they raised.

Nearly an hour had passed when he heard the sound that should not have been there.

He had paused only seconds in his mechanical polishing of a Winchester's barrel, just long enough, he judged, to establish where the sound had come from and to mark it. He waited, listening, his gaze seemingly tight and concentrated on the polishing. Had it been a footfall that had disturbed the loose wedge of rock; an animal on the prowl, a buzzard settling to its watchful perch?

Few if any animals would be on the move at this time of day in this heat. Even the lizards and rattlers were basking, and the buzzards were drifting silently.

Then it must have been a footfall.

Somebody close. Somebody who had seen him and certainly heard if not caught sight of the woman. One of Mattram's men? Not so soon, he thought. If Mattram had made even steady progress, it would be closer to sundown before he was ready to begin searching the valley.

So was somebody already here, who had been here long before the arrival of McKenna and Victoria? Somebody who had followed them from the scrub track to the creek? Somebody alone, or might there be more than one, he wondered, flourishing the polishing rag on the rifle stock?

But just who in hell would choose to be out here? Drifters, prospectors, no-good scumbags on the run? The Scatterings were a safe haven, sure enough, but only to those who wished – or were forced – to stay hidden.

It was time to call the woman, decided McKenna, get her out of that creek-bed pool and dressed; get to moving on, make for higher ground before dark.

He set the rifle aside as casually as he could summon, stood up, dusted the sand from his pants as his eyes worked frantically for a sight of something, anything, that might hint at intruders.

Nothing, not a sound, not a movement.

Damn, he cursed to himself. Question now was: dare he walk away to the pool, or should he collect the Winchester, dive for the nearest cover and trust that the action would flush the intruder into moving?

He had started to reach for the rifle when the high sun exploded, the heat haze shimmered into searing flames, the buzzards screeched and the bright white day was swamped by sudden night.

TEN

The man only ever known as Bolteye stared at the near-naked woman stranded in the creek pool, grinned hungrily at her and flicked a pebble to within an inch of her glistening cleavage.

Victoria flinched, blinked on the spout of water then glared defiantly at the man. She pushed the wet hair from her cheek and felt anxiously with her toes for a firmer footing among the grit and stones of the pool bed. Where was McKenna, she wondered, risking the merest glance to her left? What had happened back there in the rock shade?

'Well, now, ain't this just turnin' out to be one helluva day?' leered Bolteye, selecting another pebble from the scattering at his feet. 'Weeks and months – darn near years – of not so much as a sight of your fellow man; nothin' save them blink-eyed lizards and spit-faced buzzards, then, lo and behold, it's like a whole season of thanksgivin' to the Good Lord. Ain't that so, Mr Burns? What you reckon to what has been bestowed on us this blessed day? Ain't the lady somethin'?'

'Somethin',' murmured the lean, dirt-and-dust-stained man at Bolteye's back.

'Mr Burns there ain't much for words, ma'am,' grinned Bolteye. 'Saves his feelin's for action, like takin' care of that scumbag fella you got along of you back there.'

'If you've—' began Victoria, spitting water.

'No, no, ma'am,' gestured Bolteye, flicking a pebble, 'he ain't dead, leastways not yet he ain't. Can't speak for the future, o' course. That'll be up to Mr Burns.'

Victoria glared and swept another strand of plastered hair from her face. Burns spat and settled himself in the shadow.

'Yessir, ma'am, your man is kinda sleepin' deep,' quipped Bolteye. 'You needn't fret to him for a while. Meantime. . . . Ah, yes, meantime we gotta come to some sorta decision about your good self.' He grinned, squatted at the pool side and ran a mottled pebble through his fingers.

'Just who the devil are you?' bristled Victoria, almost tempted to raise herself to her full height, but thinking better of it at the last moment.

'Oh, me and Mr Burns there, we ain't nobody special, ma'am – though I daresay we're kinda special in your life right now, eh?' tittered Bolteye. 'We just drift around these godforsaken mountains, takin' what we can where and when it presents itself. Kinda like we're takin' you, ma'am.'

'If you think for one minute I'm going to agree to anything—'

'Don't matter, ma'am, we ain't fussed. You don't have to agree, you don't have to disagree. Like I say, me and

Mr Burns take what we can when it's there. And you are very definitely right there, ma'am.'

'I'm warning you—' began Victoria again.

'No ma'am, that is precisely what you ain't doin'. Only thing you got to do is, first, get yourself out of that pool before you either boil or freeze to death, and second, explain how it is a classy-lookin' lady is out here in the Scatterings along of a two-bits, rifle-totin' range man.'

Bolteye flicked the mottled pebble across Victoria's shoulder and leered the hungry grin. 'Shall we get to it?'

Victoria shivered. The once calm, cooling waters of the creek pool had chilled to an icy grip, the high sun to a ball of flame, its heat searing her neck and shoulders. She set her lips defiantly as she stiffened. 'I shall leave this pool when I please,' she snapped.

Bolteye shrugged. 'Suit yourself, ma'am. We ain't goin' no place. Matter of fact—'

'Hold it right there, Bolteye. We got somethin' real interestin' here.' Burns sauntered slowly to his partner's side, the map in his hands, his gaze narrowed on the sketched detail. 'What you make of this? Found it among the woman's clothes back there.'

'You just keep your grubby fingers off my personal property!' flared Victoria, setting a tide of ripples rushing to the side of the pool. 'What you have there has got absolutely nothing to do with you. You hear me?'

Bolteye grunted, his stare on the map deepening, narrowing, then beginning to gleam as his fingers tightened on the worn parchment.

'Know somethin', Mr Burns, if I figured this for bein''

a day to be blessed, I was wrong. Oh, yessir, I was so wrong. . . . This is a hallelujah day! Praise be to the Good Lord and no mistake! And you know why, Mr Burns? I will tell you, my friend.'

Bolteye took the map in one hand and traced the detail with an index finger. 'Now this, Mr Burns, is a very carefully drawn and detailed map of an area of these mountains known well enough to us. See, right here . . . Bonnet Peak, Two Clouds Pass, the track to the Hundred Caves. . . . It's all clear as that creek water there.' He turned his gleaming gaze on Burns. 'And what, Mr Burns, do you suppose this is all about?'

'Well,' began Burns, scratching his flaky stubble, 'I would reckon—'

'It's none of your business,' trembled Victoria in a bout of shivering. 'Put that back where you found it this minute!'

Bolteye gave her a dismissive glare and spat into the rocks. 'Only good reason why a fella would go to the trouble of drawin' a map of this godforsaken, sourmash land – specially Bonnet Peak – is 'cus he'd have somethin' to hide. Somethin', Mr Burns, to *bury*.' He grunted knowingly and slapped his partner's shoulder. 'Now what you reckon that for bein'? Why would you figure a man takin' all that trouble to trail a godforsaken track to Two Clouds Pass and the Hundred Caves? What had he to hide that was possibly goin' to be worth facin' all this sonofabitch heat, pesterin' flies and flesh-eatin' scrub? Tell me, Mr Burns, tell me.'

'Well,' said Burns, still scratching his stubble, 'it might be as how—'

'As how there's a whole hoard of somethin' buried up

there – right where that scrawled "x" marks the spot.'

'I'm coming out. Get my clothes,' ordered Victoria. 'Get them, and then I'll tell you what you want to know.'

'You sure about this, Bolteye?' muttered Burns, glancing anxiously to where Victoria sat astride the mule, her face unmoving, eyes unblinking. 'We could be walkin' into a whole hornet's nest of trouble.'

'I'd face a plague of the varmints for the prospect we got comin' up, Mr Burns,' gleamed Bolteye. 'You heard the woman. You heard what she said: the gold hoard up there is all that was taken from the raid on the bank at North Canyon. And you recall that well enough, don't you? 'Course you do. Them raiders grabbed a fortune, Mr Burns, an absolute fortune.'

'Yeah, but—'

'And if you're worryin' about what the woman's told us of Frank Mattram and his louse sittin' on our tails, forget it. I heard of Mattram, and he won't be for passin' up what's plain as the nose on your face. He'll follow the woman, won't he? He'll want us to help her to Bonnet Peak. 'Course he will. In his interests, ain't it?'

'Well, the way I'm seein' it,' began Burns, 'we just might—'

'Mattram will follow at a convenient distance, and once we've reached the gold, he'll figure on killin' the lot of us high up there at Bonnet Peak where the bodies won't never be found. That's what he'll *figure*. But we, o'course, you and me, will be a whole lot smarter. When the time comes.'

Burns rubbed a reflective hand over his stubble and stared at the woman. 'We really need her?' he mumbled.

' 'Course we do,' said Bolteye. 'Kinda insurance, ain't she – and one helluva bonus come the future, eh? Sure thing. The gold *and* the woman, Mr Burns. Think about it. Meantime, we got the two mules, we got our provisions, and we're armed. We know the trail, we know the mountains.... Hell, let's just shift, Mr Burns. Let's just go!'

'What about the scumbag back there?' asked Burns. 'What'll we do with him? You want I should make his sleep permanent?'

'Leave him. He ain't no threat, and it don't seem as how the woman's too fussed over him either. Chances are he won't survive out here, and if he does, Frank Mattram is sure to get him. Take his Winchesters and his sidearm, then we pull out. We got other places to be, Mr Burns, and a golden future comin' up!'

The trio left the creek pool and headed north an hour before sunset. They trailed in silence and no one looked back. Not even the mules.

ELEVEN

The night had deepened, the full moon settled high and round, and the wild, lonely lands of the Scatterings slid to an eerie emptiness when McKenna opened his eyes and figured for himself not being dead.

He lay silent and unmoving, breathing evenly, his senses slipping slowly to reality, his body aching, head throbbing, but with his limbs intact and working. He listened, watched what he could see of the creek, the scrub and the rocks around him. Silent, deserted; he was alone save for whatever hunted for its survival at this hour.

It was still sometime before he eventually came to a sitting position, his expression creased to a tight wince at the swelling and bruising on the back of his head. He waited some minutes, then pulled the bandanna from his neck, crawled to the edge of the creek stream and soaked the cloth in the cool, trickling flow.

'Easy, easy,' he croaked as he bathed the wound, blinked and tried best he could to focus on his surrounds.

Whoever had made the attack had helped themselves to his rifles and Colt, but had overlooked the knife in his belt and the length of rope. He had grunted, come unsteadily to his feet and staggered the short distance to the creek pool.

They had also helped themselves to the woman.

'Damn!' he cursed, wincing again as he began to picture what had happened.

How many had been here? Two distinct sets of boot prints in the soft sand at the pool; a print of the woman's naked foot. So, two attackers, he reckoned, and travelling with mules, judging by the smell of them that still lingered. Probably mountain drifters, types who came and went through the Scatterings, scavenging what they could, wherever they could find it. Not the best of company to be keeping.

He sighed, grunted, winced again and wiped the damp bandanna over his face. How long had it taken, he wondered, for the drifters to discover the map and examine it? They would probably have had no difficulty in 'persuading' Victoria to interpret all they needed to know.

His blood ran cold for a moment. Had she volunteered the information to save her skin, under threat, or had she seen the drifters as a means of getting her to the hoard of gold unscathed? Damn it, she might even have figured for the drifters being a safer bet of avoiding Mattram than anything McKenna could offer.

But if that had been her thinking, then she had looped herself into one hell of a suicidal noose.

McKenna swallowed deeply and closed his eyes.

He had seen the map, could see it now; he had scanned it, understood it. He knew the routes to Two

Clouds Pass, Bonnet Peak and the Hundred Caves. He had noted the 'x' that must have marked where the gold was hidden. He could find his way there, probably as fast as the mountain drifters. He had promised Victoria he would see her safely to Dalton. And, damn it, that was precisely what he still had every intention of doing – in spite of the woman!

He kicked a loose rock into the creek pool, heard the thudding plop and watched as the ripples lapped to the toes of his boots. All very well to resolve to follow the woman, he pondered, but what of Mattram and his boys?

He turned quickly to stare wide-eyed into the night and the sprawl and spread of heavy shadows, fearful for a moment that Mattram might even now be watching.

Nothing. Not a sound, not a movement. Only the rocks, the scrub, the mountain peaks.

He tied the bandanna at his neck, collected his hat, looped the rope across his shoulder, patted the knife at his waist and moved carefully away from the creek pool.

What chances, he mused, that Mattram had spotted the drifters, seen them trailing north with the woman, and followed? What chance he was already out there, well ahead of McKenna? Mattram would not know of the map's details, but he would sure as sun-up realize that Two Clouds Pass was to be the first objective.

Twenty minutes later McKenna had melted far into the night and the creek pool settled to its silent stillness.

'She don't say a deal, does she?' murmured Burns, watching Victoria where she rested beneath the overhang of a sprawling outcrop.

Bolteye sniffed loudly, spat deliberately over his boot, and drew heavily on the glowing cheroot. 'No need, has she?' he wheezed. 'What's there to say? She ain't goin' to open that pretty mouth of hers 'til we reach the gold. You can bet she'll have plenty to say then!'

Burns shrugged and turned his beady gaze on the softly breaking dawn light. 'No sign yet of Mattram, but he's out there. I can feel him. You know that? I can feel him. I get to feelin'—'

'I know,' said Bolteye irritably, 'you keep tellin' me, and I'm gettin' sore-headed with hearin' you. Why don't you relax, take it easy, reckon on our good fortune. Best we've ever had – ever likely to have – since we began trailin' these mountains. I'm tellin' you straight up, Mr Burns—'

Burns nudged his partner and nodded to his left. 'Thought I heard somethin',' he hissed.

'Like what, f'cris'sake?'

'Like somebody movin'.'

Bolteye listened intently for a moment, grunted, doused the cheroot and wafted the smoke to the chill morning air. 'Get the mules ready. I'll stir the woman. We're movin' – now!'

'So you heard somethin'?' frowned Burns.

'No, but we ain't takin' chances, not the way our luck's shaped of late. We're trailin' in the steps of the gods of wealth, and I ain't for pushin' them. Let's move.'

MCKENNA'S MOUNTAIN

*

Bolteye and Burns could not have known from where they had chosen to rest up that Mattram had them in view from two different angles: above the overhang and to the left.

But his orders had been specific. 'I don't want no shootin', no killin',' he told his two remaining sidekicks. 'I just want that woman to keep movin' and lead us to the gold. Simple enough. Fact that she's trailin' along of them drifters don't matter none. They'll die when the time comes.'

'And that other scumbag, what about him?' one of his men had asked. 'You ain't goin' to keep him alive much longer, are you? Hell, he's done enough damage already, and we could have had him back there at the creek. We saw him; he weren't movin'. One steady shot. . . . And that would've been the end of the rat. As it is, he'll be followin', you can bet on it.'

'Straight bullet's too good for the sonofabitch,' his companion had added moodily. 'We should string him up, or mebbe cook him like I once seen Apaches—'

'I appreciate your feelin's about the good friends we've lost,' Mattram had soothed. 'Feel the same myself, but we got more than straight retribution at stake here. A whole sight more. We got all that gold waitin' on us; a fortune, three fortunes when you come to reckon. Now, way I come to figurin' it, there ain't goin' to be no pleasure in havin' the luxury of a fortune sittin' in our laps if there's still remains of how we came by it clutterin' the scene. You follow me?'

He eyed the two men closely. 'Ain't a livin' soul goin'

to fix us to that shootin' at the stage,' he went on. 'So now we make absolutely certain of everythin' by eliminatin' the others where there ain't the remotest chance of some drifter stumblin' across their bodies, leastways not 'til they're no more than bones. And when I say others, I mean everybody: the woman, them scumbags who've hitched themselves to her, and that murderin' sonofabitch we got a personal score to settle with.'

Mattram's dark eyes had gleamed as if already seeing gold. 'And they're all goin' to die high up there in them mountains. . . .'

TWELVE

McKenna had moved at speed through the cooler hours of the breaking dawn, heading directly north and climbing higher at every opportunity of a passable track.

His aim now was to get ahead of Victoria and the drifters, keep clear of Mattram and his sidekicks and be settled at Two Clouds Pass well in advance of the others. It was not an impossible task. The drifters would be forced to hold to the lower tracks for the benefit of the mules. Mattram would almost certainly keep the woman in sight. To lose her now in the maze of ridges, creeks, gullies and peaks of the Scatterings would be a disaster. McKenna, on the other hand, was travelling light and alone, but with the added advantage over Mattram of knowing where he was going.

He had, he reckoned, the slimmest of edges.

But the going had not proved easy for limbs that were already weary, a head that refused to stop throbbing and eyes that ached to bloodshot holes in the effort of concentration. Even so, he figured for being ahead and had the Pass in his sights as the sun cleared the peaks in the east and the sky widened on its familiar cloudless blue.

He halted in the cover of a squat of boulders, ran the bandanna over his face and drank a tight swallow of water from his canteen as he scanned the terrain. More rocks, more boulders, the razor edges of ridges, the drift here and there of loose shale slopes. His gaze narrowed. But there, still at some distance at the mouth of Two Clouds Pass, was exactly what he was looking for and had prayed he might find.

He grunted his satisfaction, adjusted his hat against the steadily strengthening sunlight, and moved on, this time holding himself lower, passing quickly from cover to cover.

He halted again in shadow, peered across the glare, took stock of where he was, how far to go. Another ten, fifteen minutes, he reckoned, and he would be within reach of the lean tangles of high scrub and the twists of two parched trees.

He winced, ran his fingers over the handle of the knife as if to seek reassurance, and left the shadow for the rougher journey over scattered rocks, loose stones and deep cracks and fissures, the sun climbing ever higher in its relentless glare. The early sweat had already stained his shirt and begun to trickle to the bandanna. He slowed the pace, took stock again as he blinked the sweat clear of his eyes, then listened. No sounds. Not so much as a calling hawk.

McKenna came quickly to the two trees, dropped to one knee and laid a hand on the trunk of the tree nearest to him. Old, dry, as near dead as made no difference, he judged. The same would go for its neighbour. He ran his tongue over his lips, eased the tightness of his hat and crawled to what appeared to be the edge of the sprawl of rocks.

The drop to the pass way below began gently, easily, little more than a slope of soft dirt, broken rock and clinging scrub. But thirty feet on, it dropped sheer to the twisting trail of the pass.

Was the plan he had in mind possible, he wondered? Had he the time to put it into operation?

The pass was clear and silent enough right now, and there were no sounds or movements yet of the approaching drifters or any sight of Mattram and his men. He grunted, took a final look at the drop to the bass, and crawled back to the trees.

Time to get busy, he decided, slinging the rope from his shoulder.

Victoria twitched her shoulders to hide the surge of a sudden shiver, took a firmer grip on the rope at the mule's neck, and licked the salty sweat from her lips. Her head ached with images and swirling thoughts. . . . The map, the gold, McKenna, Mattram, and not least the two mountain scumbags trailing at her side into what seemed now an ever growing, encircling, suffocating world of stone and rock.

Had she done the right thing? Giving up the map and handing the chance to Bolteye and Burns of trekking to Bonnet Peak and the caves in search of the buried gold had kept her alive and in one as yet unmolested piece. But she was under no illusion of the prospects once the gold had been recovered.

But of McKenna? The drifters had simply left him; would he follow, or would he make his own way out of the Scatterings to Dalton? Would he avoid Mattram?

Was he reckoning even now that Victoria had sold him out in some revengeful greed for gold?

Had he not been able to see, damn it, that pandering to Bolteye's and Burns's own greed had been the price of survival?

'Two Clouds Pass comin' up, lady,' grinned Bolteye, crooking a Winchester across his body as he walked at the side of the mule. 'And once into it, we don't stop, not for nothin'. Not 'til we see the clear light at the other end. Ain't that so, Mr Burns?'

'That's just so,' called his partner from behind them.

'T'ain't no place for lingerin',' added Bolteye a touch more soberly. 'Too narrow and a whole sight too dark for comfort. You get caught in there, and it's as good as boardin' out on Boot Hill. So we don't stop. You understand, ma'am?'

Victoria murmured her understanding. 'And then?' she asked, her stare ahead unmoving. 'When do we reach Bonnet Peak?'

'Gettin' a mite impatient there, eh, ma'am?' smiled Bolteye. 'Well, I guess that's to be reckoned where gold's concerned. Seen it before. Men and women. Don't make no difference. All human when we get to it, ain't we? Why, I remember old Malley Smith—'

'When?' snapped Victoria, her stare as blue as winter's ice.

'Sometime t'morrow if our luck holds. Mules'll need restin' overnight. T'ain't no easy climb on Bonnet Peak.' Bolteye resettled the Winchester. 'Whoever carried the gold up there in the first place, sure as hell had an iron constitution.' He eyed Victoria closely for a moment. 'Care to tell me about him, lady?'

'No,' said Victoria flatly. 'It's of no concern to you or anyone else. Gold is gold and there's the end of it.' She flashed a chilling glance at the man. 'Your time would be better spent watching out for Mattram.'

Bolteye spat irritably. 'No sight of him so far,' he grunted.

'It's hardly likely he's going to announce himself, is it?' quipped Victoria.

Bolteye glared, spat again and fell back to join Burns. 'Woman's gettin' on my nerves,' he growled. 'I ain't much for keepin' her a spit longer than necessary. You in agreement, Mr Burns?'

Burns flicked a stick across the loaded mule's flank and looped the rope leading it casually across his arm. 'Way I see it – for what it's worth and the way I'm puttin' it – once I got my share of the gold up, I'll be rich enough to have m'self all the women I want. So what's one female here or there? Any amount where she came from, ain't there? Tell you straight, I've got a fancy for one of them Mexican types.'

'Yeah, well, we ain't goin' to fuss ourselves over your fancies right now. Let's just keep the gold in mind. Get to that before we come to your womanizin'.' Bolteye glanced back along the track they had followed, then scanned the higher reaches. 'Anythin' of that scumbag, Mattram?'

'Nothin',' said Burns, flicking the stick again, 'but I reckon for him bein' within sight of us. Anywhere up there,' he nodded to the higher crags. 'Just waitin' and followin'. Old Apache style. Works every time.'

Bolteye glared, spat and remained silent.

The drifters and their captive were still well short of

the entrance to the pass and could not have noticed in the next few minutes the ominous trickle of loose stone and rock that fell from the higher slopes like the start of an avalanche.

THIRTEEN

McKenna spat into his hands, took a firm grip on the broken tree branch again and attacked the dry, cracked stone and dirt beneath the boulder. He was beginning to make an impression, he reckoned. It had been a wild-card gamble, but it might yet succeed.

He worked solidly for another five minutes, then paused, stood back and breathed easily as he wiped the sweat from his face and neck, at the same time listening carefully for sounds in the pass far below him. Nothing. Still only silence. He blinked on the glare and shimmer and examined the branch. Breaking it clear of one of the dead trees for use as a digging tool had been the easy part. Digging at the base of the boulder had proved a deal more difficult and taxing.

But if he could shift just a few more inches of dirt to create a channel around the bulk, then his chances of roping it and dragging it from its resting place to crash down the slope to the sheer drop to the pass were hopeful.

An even bet, he figured, spitting into his hands again.

McKenna had noted the first trickles of dirt wriggling across the slope like snakes when he eventually paused again to clear the sweat and check that the broken branch was holding out.

He watched the dirt slither away and disappear over the lip of the slope. How distant were the drifters, he wondered, and would they notice the dirt too early for the main fall to have its impact? And what now of Mattram and his sidekicks?

He grunted, threw aside the branch and reached for the length of rope.

Minutes later, he was ready – the rope secured round the boulder, the channel cleared of loose debris, the ground smoothed best he could manage under the soles of his boots. He took up the slack, scuffed his heels into a firm footing and heaved.

'Shift, damn you!' he cursed under his breath as the palms of his hands burned on the rope. 'Shift!' A boot slewed from its anchorage. McKenna cursed, regained his balance, winced at the pain in his arms, the throb in his head.

He made one more effort, then released the rope, caught his breath, scrubbed the bandanna across the lathering of sweat, and risked a quick swig from his canteen. He stared at the boulder for a moment as if willing it to shift, grunted and took up the rope again.

'This time,' he murmured, working his heels to a footing. 'This time, in the name of. . . .'

The boulder creaked; something cracked, protested; dirt trickled and began to grow to a steady flow. McKenna heaved again until it seemed the rope must snap. He groaned, screwed his eyes to tight slits, gritted his teeth.

Another creak, another crack. More dirt. And then, without warning, the boulder rolled free and rumbled like thunder over the few feet to the edge of the slope.

McKenna watched, stooped and gasping, as the bulk gathered momentum, scooping and skidding the dirt, stones and rocks to one side, above and behind in its relentless pace. Dust clouds thickened and swirled.

McKenna coughed and spluttered, scrambled beyond their reach, the bandanna held to his mouth now as he staggered from the choking debris.

The boulder's pace quickened, its sheer weight gouging a deepening trench, the noise of it beginning to echo, lifting hawks into sudden life, sending rattlers slithering from their quiet shade.

McKenna waited, breathing heavily, the sweat like a frosted curtain across his eyes, arms loose at his sides, legs astride the scorched dirt. 'Go on!' he urged, as if the boulder might hear his plea, and then thudded a fist to the palm of his hand as the mass finally left the slope for open space and began its long descent to the pass, the tethered rope flying behind it like a swishing tail.

There were seconds then of an empty silence when it seemed the Scatterings had slipped back to sleep and only the dust clouds and wheeling hawks remained to mark the passage of the flying boulder.

The crash came with an almost deafening thud; a crack, a splintering explosion as the bulk shattered to a thousand pieces across the track.

McKenna made his slow way to the nearest shade and collapsed. But he was smiling.

'What in the name of hell's . . .' Bolteye's open mouth filled with dust and swirling dirt; a flying lump of rock clipped the top of his shoulder, forcing him off balance as he clung desperately to the rope to Victoria's mule.

'Avalanche!' yelled Burns, dragging the second mule from the debris.

'Avalanche be damned,' growled Bolteye, pulling the mule and Victoria behind him. 'That's some sonofabitch man's hand at work. You don't get . . .' He choked, gagged, spluttered. Victoria slid from the mule and pressed herself tight against the rock face.

'Came from up there,' shouted Burns, pointing to the scarred slope above the sheer drop. 'Don't see a thing now. Could've been Mattram.'

'No, not Mattram,' coughed Bolteye. 'T'ain't in his interests, is it? No, that was—'

'That scumbag we left back there at the creek? Said as how I should've finished him. You want me to do it now?'

'I don't want you to do anythin' save help me get this woman and them animals clear of this mess before the crazed fella up there gets to figurin' some other diversion. Let's shift it!'

The two drifters led the mules to the edge of the rock fall, prodding Victoria between them.

'Can we get round it?' asked Bolteye.

'Not 'til we've cleared some of these bigger pieces,' muttered Burns.

'Take an hour or more,' he mused, his gaze wandering to the walls of the pass. 'And that means the sonofabitch up there is goin' to get ahead of us. If he's seen the map and can read it, he'll know we're headin' for

Bonnet Peak.' The man spat angrily. 'Damn it, he could be waitin' for us.'

Bolteye turned savagely on Victoria, his eyes gleaming like wet black stones in his dust-caked face. 'Did that fella you were with see the map?'

'He might have,' said Victoria haughtily. 'I don't recall.'

'Well, you just get to recallin',' growled Bolteye, bringing the flat of his hand across the woman's cheek.

Victoria gasped, fell back against the mule, steadied herself and glared defiantly at Bolteye, her fingers moving softly over her cheek.

'Oh, yes,' she said coldly, 'he saw it. You bet he did! More than once. All the time. And he read it clear as day, mister. You can bet on that too! And if it is McKenna up there, I wouldn't give—'

'Shut it!' snapped Bolteye. He swung round to Burns. 'You ever heard of some two-bits range drifter name of McKenna? No, neither have I, but we sure as hell got saddled with him by the look of it!'

'So you want I should get up there, go find the rat? Wouldn't take an hour.'

'Don't be a fool,' clipped Bolteye. 'That's just what he wants us to do: be diverted, take our minds off where we're goin'. No, Mr Burns, we get through this mess fast as we can and plan on bein' through the pass come sundown.' He shielded his eyes against the glare as he scanned the crags and peaks. 'Mattram will have seen all this. He'll have figured what's happenin'. It's in his interests as much as ours to make sure this McKenna fella don't hold us up, so let's leave the sonofabitch to Mattram. What you reckon, Mr Burns?'

'I reckon we should do just that.' Burns scratched his sweat-soaked stubble. 'Let's get to it, eh?'

Victoria's fingers fell away from the weal on her cheek. She was not going to forget the blow in a hurry, she resolved, her defiance softening to a slow grin at the thought that McKenna was still with her.

The light was bright and intensely white, the heat searing and shimmering in the high afternoon sun when McKenna stirred in the slim shade at the sound of a falling rock.

His eyes opened carefully on the misted sweat; he licked slowly at his caked, cracked lips, but did not move a limb. Another sound. Same distance. A footfall. Somebody approaching. Or searching.

McKenna closed his eyes again and waited.

FOURTEEN

The shadow reached from the scant cover across the rough open ground like a crooked black arm, paused as if leaning to rest, and did not move for what seemed to McKenna, through his narrowed gaze, a full, exhausting minute. It was less by the time it shifted again, edging ever closer to the patch of shade.

Should he take a chance and make a break for it, he wondered, trust that he could put the rock cover between himself and the approaching fellow before he could use whatever weapon he was carrying? But was the fellow alone? Unlikely, he figured. This was one of Mattram's sidekicks. The other would be close, and Mattram not far behind the pair of them.

The shadow was still. The fellow watching, figuring for McKenna being either deep in sleep, or feigning it. He was not sure which.

McKenna was almost tempted to grunt his satisfaction at his efforts with the boulder, but realized it would have taken Mattram only seconds to deduce whose hand had been on the bulk. He stirred on a deeper breath and widened his gaze just enough to check on the approaching shadow. No change.

Delaying Victoria and the drifters on their trek to Bonnet Peak was one thing, dealing with Mattram would be something else. And with only a knife in his belt. Damn it, he needed a gun – any gun – and fast.

But there might be a way. . . .

'You hold it right there, fella,' called McKenna, his eyes still closed, his body relaxed. 'I ain't goin' no place, and I ain't armed, so if you're plannin' on firin' that piece you're totin' there—'

'On your feet,' ordered the sidekick, stepping into full view, a Winchester firm in his grip, his gaze narrowed but fixed and steady. 'You hear me?'

'I hear you,' sighed McKenna, struggling to his feet. He settled a lazy, dismissive gaze on the swarthy-faced, sweat-stained man. 'So what's your problem?' he asked, dusting the dirt from his shirt.

'I should finish you right where you stand, mister,' glowered the sidekick. 'You ain't no better than a dog.'

'Matter of opinion, o'course,' quipped McKenna. 'But we ain't goin' to scorch out here debatin' it, are we? Now, you've either got somethin' on your mind, or you ain't.' He adjusted his hat. 'Where's Frank Mattram?'

'Takin' a closer look at your handiwork right now, but he'll be here, don't you fret.' The man dribbled a grin. 'Got a few personal scores to settle with you, fella.'

McKenna shrugged casually, spat across a rock, his eyes working feverishly through the shadows for the second sidekick. Left, right, left again; sifting, probing for the shape. . . . There, damn it, deep in the cover of boulders, the glint of a barrel ranged very deliberately on McKenna.

No chance now of taking out the fellow facing him.

'Drop that knife you've got tucked away there,' snapped the man.

McKenna obliged, shrugged again and slung his weight to one hip. 'Wastin' an awful lot of time, ain't you?' he drawled, his eyes still working like lights in the shade of his hat brim. 'Them drifters and the woman could be long gone by the time you get to stirrin' again.' He grinned. 'Might give you the slip, mightn't they? Hell, you could lose 'em awful easy up here in these mountains. Just think, all that gold in the hands of them sonofabitch drifters. . . .'

'Shut it!' growled the sidekick. 'I ain't interested in your opinions, mister – only in seein' you stretched out for the buzzards to feed on.'

'Well, now,' began McKenna, but fell silent at the sight of Mattram looming out of the rock shadows like a sliced sliver of them.

'You been busy, mister.' Mattram smiled, twirling a long-barrelled Colt through his fingers. 'Sure as hell made a mess down there in the pass. Be a while yet before them folk get to movin'. But we ain't in no hurry, are we? Unless, o'course, you've got a pressin' matter I ain't aware of yet.'

McKenna stayed relaxed. 'You're holdin' the deck,' he mouthed on the flicker of a grin. 'Your deal.'

'Too damned right I'm dealin'!' Mattram's expression darkened. 'And I got a whole heap of arguments to settle with you, fella, not the least of which bein' them bodies of my men feedin' the crows back there.' He wiped a hand across his mouth. 'You can figure the sort of retribution I got in mind for that, can't you?'

'I can guess,' said McKenna.

'And then there's the little matter of your association with that woman and what you saw when you found her.'

'It's a consideration,' clipped McKenna.

'But of greater importance is that gold up there and gettin' to it.'

McKenna smiled. 'Now why did I figure that might be the case?'

'So what it all boils down to, mister, is this: gold first, shootin' the unwanted later.'

'I'm pleased to hear it,' said McKenna.

'Don't get comfortable. You're first in the firin' line.'

'I'd also figured that!'

Mattram turned sharply to his sidekick. 'We're pullin' out,' he called. 'We stay high and keep them mountain scum and the woman in our sights round the clock, same as before. But stay your distance.' He swung back to McKenna. 'As for this rat, rope him like a steer and we drag him with us.'

McKenna grunted quietly to himself. He still needed that gun.

It took Bolteye and Burns two long, sweating hours in the searing heat of the midday sun to clear the shattered boulder and make a crack wide enough and safe enough for the mules to proceed into the pass.

'Next time I get so much as a whiff of that McKenna fella, I'm goin' to put a bullet clean between his eyes,' Bolteye had cursed through his lather. 'And no messin'.'

'Save some of him for me!' Burns had gasped as the last of the larger rocks rolled free. 'I'd bury the sonofabitch alive – if there was enough of him left to bury!'

But for all their cursing, gasping, groaning and moaning, both men had kept a wary eye on the surrounding slopes and crags, uncertain now of just where McKenna was holed up, if he was still watching, still waiting. Or had he moved on? Might he reappear anywhere in the few treacherous miles of the pass to Bonnet Peak?

And what had happened to Frank Mattram and his men? How close were they? Surely they had heard, if not seen, the crashing boulder. They had to react. Or were they, like grey ghosts, somewhere up there in the lost, empty mountains?

The silence offered nothing, save the occasional call of a hawk.

Victoria watched the proceedings with an amused if anxious eye. Her captors had been wrong-footed, forced away from their seemingly direct and uncluttered route to the gold. The man they had left at the remote creek stream had not turned back to save his own skin. And not fallen to Mattram's guns either.

He had followed. Would he come on? What did he intend? Did he have a plan?

But her amusement at the efforts of Bolteye and Burns was tinged with her own anxiety for McKenna. There had been complete silence since the rock fall, and not so much as a shadow of his presence. She too felt a coldness at the thought of Mattram lurking among the peaks, biding his time, waiting his chance like some hungry mountain lion.

She had responded quickly to Bolteye's sudden call

to be moving. 'We gotta be out of this rat-hole before sundown,' he had croaked.

Victoria had agreed wholeheartedly. The faster the better.

Mattram's thoughts had followed the same line, except that he had no plans to move through the pass. He struck out, following the drifters above the chasm across the high rocky ground of ridges and crags, his sidekicks stumbling in his wake, McKenna doing his best to stay upright with his wrists bound and the rope leading him rarely slackening.

'We'd be makin' a whole sight faster progress if you'd release me,' McKenna had urged, holding his balance against a lurch to the left. 'Can't guarantee I'll make it roped like this.'

'So who's botherin'?' one of the sidekicks had quipped.

'Not me,' agreed his partner. 'If I had my way—'

'Nobody's interested,' snapped Mattram. 'And you, mister, will stay roped as you are 'til I say other. If you make it, you make it. If we lose you to any one of these sheer drops, so be it. End result amounts to the same thing, don't it?' His gleaming face had cracked on a cynical grin.

McKenna had simply shrugged and taken a deeper breath.

Another hour of stumbling, falling, coming upright again and trying not to notice the bruises and bleeding grazes across his arms and legs, and McKenna was finally dragged into the cover of a grouping of rocks and boulders high above the pass.

'Them drifters and the woman have holed up far end of the pass, well within our sights,' Mattram had announced. 'They won't move again 'til first light. Gettin' too dark. So we'll rest up. No fire. And we stay real quiet.' He eyed McKenna. 'And that goes for you too, mister. Not a peep out of you. Settle him over there,' he had ordered to his sidekicks.

McKenna was bundled into a corner between rocks and boulders, forced to sit down and then left as Mattram and his men huddled into a hushed conversation. Only then, when their backs were turned on him, did McKenna come to examining in detail the knotted rope at his wrists.

He was smiling again when he finally relaxed and closed his eyes.

FIFTEEN

Two of them were dead to the world, deep in sleep; only the quieter, easier-going of Mattram's two sidekicks stood guard and awake. And McKenna had been watching him like a rattler for the past half-hour.

Give it a few more minutes for the night to thicken, he reckoned, and he would be ready.

He flexed his raw wrists on the loosened and slackened rope binding them, satisfied now that his patient and persistent straining and stretching through the long, hot day had been worth it. It had taken only some painfully ratlike gnawing on the binding once dusk had settled for him to complete the job. One solid tug, and the rope would part and he would be free.

He peered through the darkness at the still sleeping shapes of Mattram and his partner. Stay that way, he thought, on a parched, biting swallow. He flexed his shoulders, ran his tongue over his gritty teeth and suncracked lips and concentrated on the sounds of the night.

There was the occasional buzz of insects, the rare,

half-muted call of a bird, the deeper, throatier sounds of the sleepers, but nothing of the drifters or Victoria.

How far away were they, he wondered? How deep into the rocks of the rough country flanking Bonnet Peak? Did they intend taking the mountain track at first light, or would they wait, maybe opt for a stand-off with Mattram? The foothills to the peak were ideal ambush country. How much of this part of the Scatterings did the drifters really know?

He took a deeper breath, relaxed again, conscious of a surge of cold sweat. His gaze narrowed on the night, the silhouetted shape of the sidekick, the towering rocks, the looming, almost suffocating bulk of the surrounding boulders. His gaze moved higher to the flat, moonlit sky where the light seemed to spread as if trickled into place.

Now, he thought, pursing his lips to a soft, hissing whistle.

The sidekick tensed at the sound, turned slowly, a frown tightening his brow. He peered hard into the darkness, eased his Winchester across his body and stepped silently across the open ground.

McKenna's eyes flicked to the sleepers, back to the approaching sidekick, the palms of his clasped hands beginning to sweat.

'Well?' murmured the sidekick. 'What's your problem?'

McKenna swallowed dramatically. 'Any chance of water?' he croaked. 'Sure could use a drink.'

The sidekick stared at him, hesitated, still frowning as McKenna continued to mouth inaudibly. 'What you sayin' there?' muttered the man bending lower. 'Can't hear a word—'

McKenna's hands had parted, snapping the rope, and were round the sidekick's throat in an instant, his legs shooting forward between the man's to crunch him into losing his balance. The sidekick groaned, lost his grip on the rifle, began to choke, then froth at the mouth as McKenna's fingers closed and tightened across flesh.

McKenna winced at the slide of the Winchester into the rocks, praying, behind the swirling images of the man's sweat-lathered face, twisted lips and bulging, bloodshot eyes, that Mattram's and his partner's sleep stayed deep.

The sidekick went limp and loose under McKenna's grip almost as suddenly as he had stiffened at the first throttling hold. McKenna supported his dead, dribbling weight for a moment, then eased the body carefully, gently to the ground.

He waited, listening, sweating, his breathing fast and deep. The sleepers slept on. He came to his feet, collected the sidekick's bandoleer and the Winchester and limped achingly into the deepest shadows.

He was a part of the night and deep into the mountains within seconds.

Victoria stirred in her fitful doze, her eyes suddenly wide and bright on the darkness, the stare deep and anxious. Something had moved, she was certain. She had almost felt it. Something close but higher, lost among the crags and rocks that stood like sentinels at the feet of the peaks.

She hesitated a moment, pulled nervously at the folds of her shirt, and crossed silently through the deeper darkness of the overhang to the clutter of boulders at the end of the pass, her gaze settling instinctively on the towering mass of Bonnet Peak.

'Up there,' she murmured to herself. Or had she dreamed the shadowy shape and movement? Her gaze scanned what she could make out of the blurred ledges, ridges, drifts, cuts and sheer rock faces as if expecting any one of them to come to sudden life with someone passing, waiting, waving.

McKenna, she wondered?

Damn it, she was willing the man into her life again!

She brushed the hair from her cheeks and froze at the soft crunch of a footfall behind her.

'Trouble?' hissed Bolteye at her ear.

She leaned away from the man's fetid breath. 'No, nothing – nothing at all,' she stammered. 'I must have been dreaming. It's kind of spooky out here.'

'Oh, yes, ma'am, it's sure as hell that – spooky, like you say.' Bolteye's gaze gleamed as he settled a firm hand on Victoria's waist. 'But, then, that's the Scatterings, ain't it? Haunted, they say. Not that you have need to worry, my dear. Not at all. Not while I'm here.'

Victoria had stiffened at the man's touch but not pulled away from the grip. 'Whatever it is you're thinking, mister, you can forget it,' she said, the voice as cold as ice. 'I am not that spooked!'

The grip tightened. Bolteye leaned closer. 'Wouldn't doubt it for a moment. You ain't come this far without knowin' where you're goin', eh? Right? You bet I'm right, lady.' He pressed his body against her. 'But seein' as how you and me have got one helluva lot of co-operatin' to do before we get our hands on that gold, I figure we should get started. Seems to me as how we got some busy times comin' up. So. . . .'

Victoria squirmed clear of the grip and closeness in a scramble of arms and legs. 'I said forget it, mister!' she seethed. 'And I meant just that.' She stood back. 'Let's get some rest. You out here; me over there. And that's the way it'll stay! Understand?'

'You tell him, ma'am,' grinned Burns, sidling out of the shadows like a tired-eyed snake. 'Needs puttin' in his place from time to time.' He spat deliberately to within an inch of Bolteye's boot. 'Ain't that so, my friend? But meantime, the lady's right: we should rest up. That's goin' to be some sonofabitch climb we got facin' us come sun-up.'

Bolteye grunted, scowled and strode away to the hitched mules.

Burns's grin faded. 'You watch your back where he's concerned, ma'am. He ain't to be trusted.'

Victoria straightened her shirt, tossed her hair and turned her gaze back to the crags and rocks. There it was again, she thought, the same movement. Nothing more than a shadow, but it had a shape. One she knew well enough.

'Never heard a thing, damn it. Never saw nothin'. How the hell did he do that? Had the sonofabitch tied like a rat in a bag.' The sidekick wiped his sweat-soaked face then pushed his hat to the back of his head.

'But not tight enough!' grunted Mattram, staring at

the body of the strangled sidekick. He kicked moodily at a loose rock, lifted his gaze to the still night-shrouded peaks and stared without blinking into the darkness. 'And now the murderin' sonofabitch is on the run again.'

'Mebbe we should go back for some help,' said the sidekick, a hand fidgeting nervously at his cheek. 'Go round up some of the boys. What you say, Frank? Day's ride and we could be in Dalton. Got m'self a good friend there, old Sammy Wishart. Him and his brothers would ride with us, 'specially if they knew there was a payout in gold. And they ain't fussed none about—'

'Don't be a fool,' growled Mattram, still staring into the darkness. 'Time we got back into these mountains them scumbag drifters and that whorin' woman'd be long gone. That range-rider with 'em, if he hadn't already put a bullet down their throats and scooped the gold for himself.' He blinked and ground his teeth noisily. 'We're stayin'. We're goin' on, beginnin' right now, and we're goin' to get that murderin' sonofabitch before noon, or my name ain't Frank Mattram.'

'But Frank,' protested the sidekick, 'that fella's gettin' the better of us at every turn. Damnit, he's taken out darn near every last one. . . .' The man gulped and began to sweat again. 'I ain't so sure, Frank, as how I want to go on. I mean, not like this. We need men; we need guns. . . .'

Mattram turned a slow, steady gaze on the man. 'You sayin' as how you ain't goin' on? You callin' this the end of the line?'

'Well, I ain't exactly sayin' as how—'

'Seems to me like you are,' quipped Mattram. 'And

there ain't a deal at fault with my hearin'.' His glare deepened. 'Well, now, here's a situation. You sayin' as how you're goin' to just walk outa here and scuff your boots all the way to Dalton town? You tellin' me that, f'cris'sake? And what you plannin' on doin' when you get there? You goin' to come back for me, ridin' along of your *good friends*? That it? I think not. No, no, I definitely think not.'

'Hell, Frank, I wasn't sayin' as how I'm desertin' you—'

'Too right you ain't!' growled Mattram, his Colt suddenly clear of its holster, levelled and steady. 'You ain't goin' no place, fella. You're stayin' right here. You're goin to help me cover our brave companion here so's them thievin' buzzards don't get to peckin' out his eyes, then we're goin' after that murderer, and when we get him—'

'You got it, Frank,' gestured the sidekick, stepping back. 'Just as you say. I ain't goin' no place. You got my word. We'll get that sonofabitch, see if we don't.' He swallowed. 'Let's get busy, eh?'

Mattram grinned and holstered the Colt with a determined thrust. 'Yeah, see if we don't,' he mouthed, his gaze beginning to gleam.

SIXTEEN

Bolteye led the reluctant mule along the rock-strewn track, watching each tentative step as if expecting it to be the last. He murmured soothingly to the animal, staring deep into its eyes at the merest hint of a gleam of panic, almost unaware, it seemed, of Victoria struggling for her own footholds a yard behind him.

'Ain't goin' to get these beasts much higher,' called Burns, leading the second mule. 'Best get 'em settled some place and come back for 'em later.'

'Need 'em for humpin' the gold, Mr Burns,' sweated Bolteye. 'We ain't goin' to be able to carry that out of the Scatterings, are we?'

'Kind of assumin' a lot there, I'd reckon,' answered Burns, clicking his tongue to encourage his mule. 'We ain't seen no gold yet; we can't be certain there is any gold, and we sure as hell ain't got a sniff of a clue how much there is. Not unless you can help us on that, ma'am.'

'I've no idea,' retorted Victoria dismissively.

'That was some raid them fellas pulled at North Canyon,' said Bolteye, halting for a moment to mop his brow. 'And I've been thinkin' about it these past hours, tryin' to recall what happened all that time back. 'Tain't easy. Memory don't serve me that well, but I reckon them Pendrick brothers were generally thought to be the ringleaders of the gang.'

'Yeah, that's so,' agreed Burns, with a sidelong glance at the suddenly pale-faced Victoria. 'There was Fred, Charlie and the younger one, Sam. But they weren't the only ones. There were others.... Kid Sloane, he was with 'em. And what about Jack Cutchean?'

'Too right, Mr Burns,' agreed Bolteye. 'But there was one who got clean away and was never heard of again. Now who the devil—'

'I don't see that it matters after all these years,' snapped Victoria irritably. 'It's what they took that interests us, not who took it. And in any case, they're probably all dead by now.'

'Reckon you could be right at that, ma'am,' said Bolteye, blinking on the sun glare.

'But one fella did get away,' persisted Burns. 'And I'd figure for him bein' the one who carted the gold up here. Somebody must have. So who was he, and what in hell happened to him?'

'Don't matter none,' grunted Bolteye. 'Let's do like you said, Mr Burns, and get these mules settled some place. Then we climb higher.'

Victoria sighed and fanned a hand across her glistening face. There had been no movements, no shapes or sounds among the crags. Nothing, in fact, save a cruising buzzard.

Stay close, if you're up there, McKenna, she thought.

McKENNA'S MOUNTAIN

*

'Mebbe we should be gettin' closer,' muttered the sidekick, his body flat and spread-eagled across the rocks where he lay like a basking lizard. 'They ain't goin' at any sort of pace down there. Looks now as if they've left the mules.'

Sweat dripped from the man's stubble as Frank Mattram crawled to his side and peered into the rocks and twist of track far below.

He studied the situation for a while, narrowing his gaze in his glances to left and right, then pointed ahead to the mass of Bonnet Peak and a cluster of giant boulders where the track climbed out of sight.

'There,' he murmured. 'That's where we'll make the first strike – in the cover of the boulders. We take out just one of them mountain drifters. Choice is yours, but make it the first in your sights. No messin'. No hesitation. But we don't harm the woman. I want her in one untouched piece – with the map.'

'You got it, Frank, leave it to me,' grinned the man.

Mattram's gaze moved through a slow, studied arc, pausing to probe the morning's deepening shadows, examine the rocks as if taking them apart layer by layer, moving on again; searching for whatever only he would know should not be there. 'No sign of that scumbag,' he croaked almost to himself. 'Must be gettin' thirsty by now.'

'Let him fry,' said the sidekick. 'We'll get to him soon enough. Deal with the drifters first.'

Mattram's gaze continued to move steadily through the rocks and shadows. 'He's out there. I can feel him, damn it.'

'Don't let him get to you, Frank. He ain't worth it.'

'Killed enough of us, ain't he? Snuffed out my men like they were no more than dust. And you can bet he's figurin' he ain't done yet.' Mattram was silent for a moment. 'That's what worries me,' he added grimly.

The sidekick said nothing.

'We'll rest up in the cover there, ma'am. There'll be some shade in them boulders.' Bolteye pointed along the twisting shelving track to where it narrowed into the rock mass. 'Give ourselves a break, eh? We're doin' well enough. What you reckon, Mr Burns?'

'We rest up, but no longer than we have to.' Burns glanced anxiously round him. 'Kinda spooks me up here knowin' we ain't alone. I ain't much for it.'

'Well, don't you fret none, my friend,' returned Bolteye, lending a hand to Victoria. 'We ain't none of us for claimin' this is bluegrass country. That it surely ain't. We'll be clear of it just as soon as we've attended to our business.' He smiled wetly at Victoria. 'By which I mean as soon as the lady's attended to *her* business.' His smile gleamed. 'Don't want no misunderstandin's here.'

'There'll be no misunderstandings, you can be sure of that,' said Victoria icily. 'I can guarantee it.'

'I knew that, ma'am,' beamed Bolteye on a rattling wheeze. ' 'Course I did. You wouldn't be for leadin' a fella astray, would you? Show your decent appreciation, wouldn't you?' His smile twitched and expired. 'Like the generous share of that gold hoard you're plannin' on givin' us.'

Victoria paused in the struggle for her next foothold.

'Generous?' she frowned. 'How *generous* are we talking of here?'

Bolteye lodged a boot firmly on a rock and steadied his weight on one knee. 'Well, now, that's another thing I been givin' some thought to, and it seems to me—'

'Seems to me,' said Burns, heaving his frame alongside his partner, 'that we should get to seein' the gold before we start countin' it out. Who's to say there's any gold up there, f'cris'sake?' he went on, catching at his breath. 'Who's to say somebody ain't beaten us to it?' He turned his gaze on Bolteye. 'Who's to say that fella you say got clean away and weren't seen again didn't make his way back here to where he'd stashed the hoard and simply helped himself? You can't be certain . . .'

The rifle shot cracked like a steel blade splintering bone-dry rock.

Burns writhed in agony, his hands locked round his thigh, sweat lathering his face and neck. 'Bolteye,' he moaned. 'Do somethin', f'cris'sake!'

The second shot spat with equal venom, spinning Burns round like a top where he lay. He half screamed, groaned, twitched again, but was already dead from the blast into his chest as his body skidded and slid down the track under the momentum of its own weight.

Bolteye gulped as he watched the body tumble from sight somewhere in the crags below, a sheer drop from the track. 'Hell,' he moaned, blinking on his blurred, swimming vision. 'Sonofa-goddamn. . . .' But he choked on his curse and swung round to Victoria. He pressed himself to her side in the narrow gap between the rocks. 'Mattram or your range-ridin' friend?' he croaked.

Victoria merely swallowed and shook her head, her gaze scanning madly over the crags she could see.

'Don't matter a cuss, anyhow,' he grunted. 'Mr Burns ain't one bit fussed. He's buzzard meat.'

Victoria shivered. 'We can't stay here,' she hissed, stifling a retch at the smell of Bolteye's sweating closeness. 'We must move. Go higher. Go back. . . . Something.'

'Oh, sure,' quipped Bolteye. 'Minute we step from this cover, one of us is dead. Very likely me. And I ain't for joinin' Mr Burns in a hurry.'

'So what do we do?'

Bolteye narrowed his gaze on the shimmering haze of the rocks. 'We wait,' he murmured. 'We sit this one out, lady. We don't go nowhere and we don't move a muscle.'

'You never said a truer word, my friend,' mocked Frank Mattram from behind the glinting barrel of a levelled Winchester at their backs.

SEVENTEEN

'Been a long time, my dear,' sneered Mattram, probing the rifle barrel into Victoria's midriff as he pushed her into the deeper shade and cover of the boulders. 'Now, let me see, when was it we last had a cosy hour together?'

'We have never had a cosy hour together,' croaked Victoria on a parched, dust-dry throat. 'And I would never want—'

'Bannenfield,' clipped Mattram, with another probe of the rifle.

'Bannenfleld it was, boss,' agreed the sidekick, ranging his own Winchester on Bolteye's sweat-soaked gut. 'The Five Stud Palace. Recall it like it was only yesterday.'

Victoria grimaced at the gritty harshness of the rock surface through her shirt, glanced quickly at Bolteye stranded like a beached whale under the sidekick's watchful gaze, and then into the high, cloudless blue above the crags and peaks.

'Charlie Pendrick, Jack Cutchean . . .' muttered Mattram through a slow grin. 'Yeah, I remember, 'course I do. But I also remember somethin' else, don't I, lady? You know I do! Somethin' I should've found when I took that stage apart.' The grin slid away, the levelled Winchester tightened. 'The map, lady, the map.'

'Go to hell!' flared Victoria.

'Hear the lady there, will you?' mocked Mattram. 'Just hear her. Anybody might think she was doin' the dealin' here. And her, no better than a two-bits bar whore.' His face darkened as if on the passing of a shadow. 'I know you have it, lady. You wouldn't be here if you hadn't. And neither would this louse of a mountain drifter.'

Mattram lowered the rifle, stood back and relaxed. 'We can do this quick and easy, or quick and messy. Hand over the map, lady, and there's the end of it. Get stubborn and I'm goin' to have to take if from you. And that could get painful – for this fella, too.'

'Give him the map, f'crissake!' blurted Bolteye through his lathering of sweat. 'He's goin' to get it, anyhow.'

'You want I should silence this rat, Frank?' said the sidekick, glaring into Bolteye's face.

'I'll count to three,' grinned Mattram. 'One. . . . Two. . . .'

'All right,' snapped Victoria, unbuttoning her shirt with a flourish to produce the map. 'Have it, damn you!' She handed the folded sheet to Mattram, ran her tongue over her lips and gazed into the peaks.

'So what's the deal?' blustered Bolteye, blinking furiously. 'You've got the map – and, hell, you can have the woman – but what about us? What about *me*?'

The sidekick spat in disgust. 'You want my opinion—' he began.

'You don't figure none, fella,' said Mattram, folding the map carefully into his vest pocket. 'So I guess you ain't needed. You got any place to be?'

'What the hell you sayin' there,' blustered Bolteye again. 'Hell, you've just shot my partner, and we'd been t'gether for years, and now you're askin' if I got some place to be! The hell I have! Only place I wanna be—'

'We're wastin' valuable time,' quipped Mattram.

'Hold it!' floundered Bolteye, wiping a hand over his face. 'You're goin' to need me. Sure you are. How you goin' to shift that hoard up there? Just the two of you ain't goin' to do it, and the woman here ain't goin' to be no help, is she? Hell, no. You need me, and them mules we got hitched back there.'

'He's got a point, Frank,' murmured the sidekick. 'Mebbe we could use another pair of hands, leastways for the time bein'.'

Mattram drummed his fingers over the rifle stock, his stare moving between the lathered gaze of Bolteye, the pale, withdrawn expression on Victoria's face, and the gleaming, shimmering rocks.

He grunted, swung the Winchester to his shoulder and had taken a step back towards the rocky track when the shot rang out, whined and lifted a clutter of buzzards into the cloudless blue.

Victoria's scream was lost on her gasp; Bolteye slid to his butt where he stood with his back to a boulder; Mattram ducked, half-turned and glared like an angered lion into the crags. It was some moments and a second shot later before anyone noticed the sprawled, bleeding body of the sidekick.

'Is he dead?' croaked Bolteye, not daring now to move.

Victoria shivered and looked away.

Mattram stared at the lifeless body, then squinted against the glare as he scanned the higher reaches.

'Sonofabitch,' he muttered drily. 'Sonofa-goddamn-bitch! Took him out with one shot.' He grunted, spat, gritted his teeth and swung his rifle into his shoulder, releasing a blaze of wild, spitting shots aimed at nothing save the equally lifeless sprawl of rocks.

'Wastin' your time and valuable lead there, mister,' groaned Bolteye, heaving himself back to his feet, the sweat dripping like dew from his chin. 'We both know who fired that shot, don't we? Don't have to have him announce it, f'crissake. It's that plains-ridin' sharpshooter who somehow got himself attached to the woman here.'

'What do you know about him?' spat Mattram, pulling Victoria round to face him. 'I know damn well where you got tied in with him, but who is he? Where'd he come from?'

Victoria tidied her shirt across her shoulders without looking at Mattram. 'I have absolutely no idea who he is, or where he hails from,' she said as dismissively as she could summon. 'I only know him as McKenna.'

Mattram raised a hand as if to strike her, thought better of it and swung back to Bolteye. 'Must be your lucky day,' he quipped cynically. 'You get to live. Goin' to need you, aren't I? But that don't mean to say—'

'Yeah, yeah,' said Bolteye, waving an arm loosely, 'I know what you're goin' to say and, frankly, I ain't fussed one bit. We only got two choices here, mister, and neither of 'em guarantees a spit's worth of life unless we get real smart – both of us, workin' t'gether, trustin' to each other. You get me? We either go on, up there to the Hundred Caves, or we turn back. Either way, this McKenna fella's goin' to be followin'.'

Victoria stifled a half smile. Mattram grunted again and continued to scan the peaks. 'Somewhere up there,' he mused quietly. 'Somewhere. . . . Damnit, I had the fella in my hands. Should have shot him then. Now, he's taken out every last one of my men.'

'Ain't doin' no good standin' here,' said Bolteye, dusting his dirt-stained pants. 'What's the plan? We goin' on, or headin' back? Could be on the plains again in two days. There's a shortcut if we can find it.'

'We're goin' on.' Mattram wiped his forearm across his mouth. 'I ain't come this far, waited this long, lost all these men to get to bein' yellow-bellied now. Charlie Pendrick owes me. Promised me I'd be in on this. Well, he damn well should have kept his word 'stead of double-crossin' me like he did.' His gaze burned into Victoria. 'And as for this two-bits whore—'

'We don't touch her,' ordered Bolteye, his confidence returning. 'This McKenna fella won't be for takin' risks while she stays breathin'. He ain't no fool. But he don't give a damn about us, so we stay wide-awake, do this t'gether. You wanna get your hands on the woman you do that *after* we've got the gold.' He adjusted his hat. 'Leastways, that's my thinkin',' he added quietly.

'Don't you get for thinkin' you're runnin' this show, mister,' sneered Mattram. 'Just 'cus I ain't got my men around me no more don't mean you got some upper hand here. And when it comes to a share of the gold—'

'*If* it comes to a share-out of the gold,' clipped Bolteye. 'Meantime, let's clean up here before that plainsman gets to devisin' some new avalanche or puts either one of us in his sights.' He glanced quickly into the peaks. 'We've still got a long climb.'

Mattram turned to Victoria. 'And you keep to the pace, you hear? First time I catch you slackin'. . . .'

His voice dried like a spit on hot rock at the trickle of stones and pebbles that worked its way in an eerie flow between the boulders.

'He's there,' murmured Bolteye.

Mattram twitched his shoulders.

Victoria did nothing this time to stifle her smile.

EIGHTEEN

McKenna climbed quickly, hand over hand, foothold to foothold, like a four-legged mountain animal who knows his natural country by instinct.

He had waited high above the sprawl of boulders until Mattram, Bolteye and Victoria had finally moved on, then slid back to the track and made his way to where the mules had been left to await Bolteye's return with the gold.

His luck, as he had prayed, had held: the drifters had left a spare canteen of water. He had slaked his thirst, cooled his brow and neck, slung the canteen to his shoulder and with the Winchester tight in his grip, set off again for the peaks.

Getting ahead of Mattram had not been difficult. McKenna's route to the looming mass of Bonnet Peak and the Hundred Caves had been more difficult, but, given the skill and confidence to tackle the rocks and hazardous crags, a whole sight faster, bringing him a shadowy distance far above the others long before the sun was beginning to dip away to the west.

He had halted, waiting in the coolest shade for the

aches in his limbs to calm, his head to stop spinning, his mind to take sensible stock of where he was and where he planned to be.

He had successfully reduced the stage raiders to just Mattram and the drifters to one; neither, he was certain, would make a move to kill the woman yet. The hoard of gold was still the single objective for which, if it came to it, both men would sell their souls. Victoria had provided the map and for the moment was there, another hand to help when the time came. But she was also a woman; a prize, a bonus to add to the hoard. Perhaps not to be willingly disposed of in the less heady light of another day.

And she had a flair for survival among men! It would pay her captors to still watch their backs, thought McKenna, on a rueful smile to himself. The glitter of gold could easily blind a man to the loaded gun waiting in the shadows.

McKenna had been climbing again within the hour.

Bolteye settled a flat, wet hand on Victoria's butt and pushed her to the safety of the higher rock shelving.

'Never took you for no bar gal, lady,' he wheezed through a leering smile, 'but can sure see how you came to be one!' He tittered and grabbed wildly for a hold as Victoria seethed, glared back at him and pulled clear of his hand. 'Only tryin' to be helpful, ma'am. I ain't for gettin' too close.'

'You bet on it!' snapped Victoria, the sweat staining deep into her shirt.

'Leastways, not yet,' added Bolteye, drawing himself into the rocks.

'Cut the banter and save your breath,' growled

Mattram, climbing on to draw level with them. 'Let's keep concentrated on what we're doin'.' He glanced anxiously round him, his eyes narrowing as the shadows began to lengthen. 'Any sign of McKenna?' he croaked.

'We ain't goin' to see no more of him this day,' said Bolteye, releasing the sticky grip of his hatband. 'But he's around – restin' if he's got any sense. Light fades fast up here. We need to be settled safe by full dark.' He settled his hat with a thrust and stared into the higher peaks. 'The Hundred Caves and gold by this time t'morrow . . .' he murmured softly.

Victoria shuddered under the sudden chill of the sweat.

Mattram tightened his gaze on the peaks. 'I ain't for havin' that fella around when we get higher. He could make things difficult. What say—'

'I say we don't even think it, mister,' glared Bolteye. 'Up here, in the dark, hearin' things, watchin' your back like you had a ghost under your shirt? I think not.' He spat into the rock maze far below him. 'If one thing's for certain, it's that McKenna knows these mountains well enough, and mebbe this one in particular. He's been among 'em before. He knows where he is, how to handle it, and, more to the point, knows where he's goin' and where we're headin'.' He spat again, watching the fount of spittle shimmer on the light. 'Seen the map, ain't he? Read it like it was the palm of his own hand. I ain't fooled none. Ask the woman here. She'll tell you.'

Victoria stiffened. 'Of course, he's seen it,' she offered under Mattram's icy gaze. 'But that's your problem, not mine.'

Mattram's hand moved instinctively to the butt of his Colt.

'Don't be a fool,' clipped Bolteye. 'Shootin' off that piece up here could start a whole crazy fall of rock. You move quiet and real slow when you get this high. Best remember that, fella.'

'Don't get lippy,' sneered Mattram, his fingers still fluttering over the gun butt. 'I don't like lippy company.'

'Know your trouble, Mr Mattram?' sighed Bolteye leaning back on his elbows. 'I'll tell you: you figured for all this bein' an easy ride surrounded by your guns, but it ain't worked out quite like that, has it? You've lost your sidekicks and you're left with just me and the woman. And you can't afford to get rid of either of us. And then there's the gold, the fever of it. Oh, yes, there's that, eatin' into you, lurin' you like it's got you in some sorta trance.' He grimaced. 'I seen it before. It can drive a poor soul into madness.'

Mattram's mouth had opened on a threatened tirade of anger, when he froze where he stood at the sound and then the sight of another trickle of rocks and pebbles from the higher reaches.

'Keepin' busy, ain't he?' mouthed Bolteye on a slow, cynical grin.

Victoria watched the final flare of the sunset, the lunge of shadows to the enveloping darkness, pulled the collar of her shirt into her neck and settled down to wait.

But for how long, she wondered, blinking to adjust her eyes to the gathering night? Mattram and Bolteye were already relaxed in the rocks, their watchful gazes beginning to edge towards dozing, their breathing easier, levelled. She would need to wait until they were almost asleep before making her move. By then the night would be thicker, the shadows cast by the moonlight longer and deeper.

But would they sleep, or would one of them keep watch? Not a deal to watch, she thought. McKenna would have climbed higher, found his own comfortable cleft, or maybe reached one of the caves. He would not make another move, she reckoned, until first light.

She shivered as the air began to thin, and shifted her gaze to the blur of the vague track leading into the peaks. There would be little enough of it to follow even in daylight, practically nothing by night. But it was worth a try. It had to be. If she could reach McKenna, at least let him know she was free of Mattram and Bolteye, together they might just. . . .

Bolteye coughed, grunted, scraped a boot over rock. Mattram's eyes gleamed for a moment, pierced the darkness to left and right, watched Victoria through a fleeting glance, then darkened.

Into a doze or into sleep?

Victoria made an exaggerated pretence of snuggling into the chilling comfort of the rocks, folded her arms and rested her head, her eyes narrowed to slits.

She would give it what she judged to be fifteen minutes, then move.

Victoria slipped across the darkness in silence, reached the blur of the track, paused to check that Mattram and Bolteye were still dozing, and stepped tentatively on to the next safe hold.

It had been closer to the half-hour before she had summoned the courage to make the move, but now, with the darkness wrapped around her like a cloak, the moon watching like an eye, the air cool across her cheeks, she felt certain of the way, confident of making contact with McKenna.

She reached again, found a grip and heaved herself higher, a few more feet clear of the sleeping men. She caught her breath, gulped on the fresher air, licked at a sparkling of cold sweat, climbed on. The rock shapes seemed to clamour, gathering round her like a curious crowd, mocking her, watching, touching, feeling.

She paused, conscious now of the strain on her limbs, the ache of concentration behind her eyes, the first whispers of her own doubt. Supposing McKenna had moved fast enough to reach the Hundred Caves, climbed far out of her reach, beyond any hope of her joining him. What if she were to lose herself in the maze of crags and rocks? What if she fell?

She had shuddered and clambered into the next ridge when the hand clamped on her ankle, tightened and locked cold fingers into a vicious grip.

'Goin' some place, lady?' spat Mattram.

Victoria turned her head slowly to stare into the man's glinting gaze. She tossed her hair defiantly. 'Can't a woman have some privacy round here?' she quipped.

'Not goin' that way, she can't. Get yourself down here. I got somethin' to discuss with you.'

Victoria glanced despairingly into the darkness above her, the moonlit shapes of the higher peaks, sighed and struggled down to Mattram's side. 'I have nothing to discuss with you,' she mouthed coldly.

'We'll see,' said Mattram. He waited, glancing quickly back to the snoring Bolteye, then fixed his blade-sharp gaze on Victoria's face. 'We've got somethin' we both need to discuss. The gold stashed up there.'

'Forget it,' sneered Victoria. 'Everything's been said on that subject.'

'I think not.' Mattram scrubbed a hand over his stubble. 'I know all about how you came into Charlie Pendrick's hands, and I know for sure you didn't wed him. Not you! Nossir, never reckoned you for that.' His stare tightened and narrowed. 'But you were smart enough not to object to the old rat trustin' the map to you for safe-keepin', and you didn't waste no time in lookin' to your own interests back there at the stage. And then gettin' still smarter when you hitched yourself to that two-bits plainsman who seems to have a pretty shrewd understandin' of mountains – not to say how to go about killin' men!'

Victoria merely grunted and looked away to the darkness.

'Now I ain't for guessin' what you had planned once you got your hands on that hoard, but I ain't in no doubt, lady, that the situation's changed somewhat. You're fast gettin' to be on your own. And once me and that sleepin' drifter have taken out McKenna – which we will do, you bet to it – well, then the way I see it, it's comin' down to you and me. So what say we make a pledge on it right now?'

Victoria turned a cynical gaze on Mattram's

gleaming face. 'Meaning what precisely?' she asked.

'Meanin' as how we use the drifter to help us shift the gold back to the mules. Once that's taken care of, we finish him up here, leave him along of McKenna to the buzzards, and we trek south. Together. Partners. And who knows, time might come—'

'I think I heard a movement up there,' said Victoria brusquely. 'Perhaps you should go take a look.'

Mattram had grunted and turned to climb higher when the round, gleaming face grew in the light like a moon. Bolteye grinned and winked.

NINETEEN

McKenna wiped the back of his hand across his mouth, judged the distance of the leap carefully, felt for the firmness of the rock beneath his boots and launched himself into the faint dawn light like a bird.

There was a rush of chill morning air at his cheeks, a stinging bite behind his eyes, seconds when it seemed rather than clearing the chasm between the ridge and the plateau on the far side, he was falling into it. His arms spread like wings, the fingers of one hand fanned wide, the other gripping the Winchester. His legs raced on space, his body tensed.

For a moment he wanted to call out to release the tension, and then he felt the shuddering thud as he landed, the skidding slide on his back, heard the clatter and echoing crash of loose rocks, came to a breathless halt pinned against a boulder, and heaved a long, wheezing sigh of relief.

'Made it!' he croaked, opening and closing his eyes on the streaks and patches of light. He struggled to his feet, took a new grip on the rifle and concentrated on the sounds of the emerging new day. Nothing of

Mattram, the drifter or Victoria. Either they were still resting up, or climbing like slow, silent insects.

He turned and lifted his gaze to the vague shape of the mass of Bonnet Peak, what could be seen at this hour of the narrow ledge tracks, perilous ridges, overhangs and jawline of craggy levels where the rocks had grown, it seemed, like molars.

Higher still were the black holes of the Hundred Caves, each one staring as if to warn the approaching climber to stay his distance. McKenna twitched on a sudden coldness, swallowed, concentrated on his recollection of the map and the 'x' that must have marked the cave where the gold had been stashed. His gaze tightened in the effort of what he could identify against the shadowy light. More to the left, the right? Had the mark been higher, lower? How accurate was the map? Who had made it?

'Damn,' he cursed under his breath, it was too early and he was still too distant to be certain of exactly where to climb next, but he would go on to the first of the ledge tracks and the start of the caves.

He shouldered the rifle, turned again and took the few steps to where he had crossed the chasm. It would be at least another hour, he reckoned, scanning the drop to the rocks below, before Mattram got this far. He would probably skirt the chasm to the west, making it closer on midday before he had the ledge tracks and caves within his reach.

McKenna moved away. Time for Mattram to be reminded of who was still ahead of him.

'I heard every word that scumbag mouthed,' groaned

Bolteye at Victoria's back as they climbed into the rocks, Mattram leading the way some yards ahead. 'And nothin' surprised me one spit.' He spat to emphasize his disgust. 'No more than I'd have figured of the rat.'

Victoria stayed silent, her gaze concentrated on the rocks, the threatened heat in the rising sun, the shape of the man in front of her.

'That's what gold does for you, ma'am.' Bolteye cursed quietly as his boot slipped on a rock. 'Seen it all before. But that rat ain't even had a sight of gold yet. Imagine what he'll be like when we reach them caves!'

Victoria raised her gaze to the mass of Bonnet Peak, its highest reaches emerging slowly through the morning mist like muscles, the cave mouths as black as bruises.

Bolteye climbed closer to Victoria's side. 'We'd both better watch our backs. I wouldn't rate that two-bits gunslinger to a can of worms. What you reckon, ma'am? You and me goin' to stick t'gether? It's our best chance if we're goin' to come out of this alive. That rat'll shoot us in the back soon as look at us. I ain't foolin' none.'

'You're probably right,' murmured Victoria, 'but there's not a deal we can do about it right now, is there? We must carry on, be as normal as we've ever been, and maybe trust that Mr McKenna—'

'Him!' sneered Bolteye. 'You reckon we can trust McKenna any more than we can Mattram? What marks him out any better than the gunslinger? Hell, where gold's concerned—'

'What makes you suppose I can trust you?' snapped

Victoria. 'Why should I? You're in this for what you can get out of it for yourself. Perhaps you aren't any different from Mattram.'

'That ain't so, ma'am,' hissed Bolteye, struggling still closer. 'I lost my best friend back there. I got scores to settle, but I ain't for spendin' no more years sweatin' in these mountains. They can go to hell! I'm for some luxury life. Spend some money. Have me some fine clothes and good-lookin' company along of me — specially yourself, ma'am. Now I figure for us—'

'What the hell you two got so much to mutter about?' glowered Mattram, turning his gleaming, sweat-soaked gaze on the climbers behind him. 'You stay silent, you hear? No more talkin'. Save your breath, and keep your eyes skinned for that plains' vermin. He's got to show sooner or later, damn him!'

'Gettin' edgy, ain't he?' grinned Bolteye. 'Fella's gettin' to him. That's goin' to give him fidgety fingers. Might get to shootin' at his own shadow before long, so watch it, eh, and stay close?'

Victoria sniffed. Not that close, she hoped! She climbed on, disregarding the grope of Bolteye's helping hand.

McKenna worked his way through the massed rocks and boulders like an animal on the hunt. He slid from the faceless, unremitting glare of the morning sun to the cooler but still clinging shadows of the crags and spilling slopes at the foot of the final climb to the caves. This, he knew better than he knew his own body, was going to be the toughest part of the climb, with the heat gathering like fire above him, the rocks beginning to bake and even the shade to sweat.

He halted, balanced over shimmering stones, dampened his bandanna from the canteen, tied it at his neck, and narrowed his gaze on the brightness. He had opted now to make for the two larger caves some hundred feet or so to the left of where a narrow ledge could be reached from this approach. Either one of them could be the cave marked on the map, he reckoned, but now he was judging the position from what those carting the stolen hoard must have seen and debated all those years back.

It would have taken at least two of the initial gang of raiders to handle the gold this far, and by then, given the long ride out of North Canyon, the threat of pursuit, they must have been close to exhaustion. One, or perhaps both of them had decided on the Hundred Caves deep in the heart of the Scatterings as being the resting place for the time being of their precious haul. The day would come, as the heat of the raid cooled and the gang dispersed, when they would be back. . . .

McKenna grunted. This far, he pondered, perhaps on a morning very like today; the sun like a fireball, the sky cloudless, the shadows as black as night, Bonnet Peak and the Hundred Caves luring the men on. Gold would be buried that day, its exact location known to only two men, one of whom would fix the position for all time on a hurriedly scratched map.

McKenna stiffened, the sweat beading on his brow. One man had drawn the map . . . one man. . . . What had happened to his partner? Had both men survived, or had only one made it out of the mountains?

McKenna shouldered the Winchester and continued

to edge his way through the rocks and boulders, working ever closer to where he could make out the start of the smoothest climb to the ledge. He would be in the caves in an hour, he reckoned. Mattram by then would still be following, leaving McKenna time to search, take new stock, figure out. . . .

He had crunched a boot across bone before becoming aware of it, then halted instantly, not moving, hardly breathing. Long, silent seconds elapsed before he finally blinked, looked down and stared into the whiter, cracked skull of a man, the bones of his body and limbs preserved as he had fallen to the thrust of the knife blade lodged in his rib cage.

McKenna swallowed, his gaze steadying now on the detail of the skeleton: the feet, the shaped toes, one twisted and broken; the fingers flat, the thumb of the left hand slightly crooked as if about to acknowledge something or someone; the skull with its misshapen teeth, chipped eye-sockets that seemed, in the glaring sunlight, to be staring into a timeless distance.

McKenna squatted, took the knife delicately between his fingers, drew it from the ribs and slipped it into his belt. He paused a moment, studying the bones, then lifted the skull from the body and placed it with the sun at its back on a rock overlooking the way he had trekked.

For the first time in years it had something to watch for.

TWENTY

Bolteye groaned inwardly, screwed his eyes to tight slits and decided there was going to be only one way of ridding the world of Frank Mattram: he, Bolteye, was going to have to shoot him, here in the Scatterings, in the back if need be. As many shots as it took. And to hell with the noise. If it drew McKenna out of cover, all to the good. Mattram just simply had to die.

They would thank him when it was done. See the sense of it. Damn it, the woman owed the sonofabitch nothing, and McKenna would already have figured Mattram's plan: the gold and the woman for himself, but if it came to it, the gold took priority.

And there was another very good reason. Bolteye reckoned he could work along of McKenna when it came to shifting the hoard, do it without having to watch his back every few seconds. McKenna could be trusted. He was nobody's fool, but he was no double-dealing gunslinger either. He would see the woman and the gold safely out of the mountains and back to the plain. He was that sort of a man, he reckoned. He had a code and was not for breaking it.

And he maybe had a warm eye for the woman.

Bolteye took a firmer grip on his rifle, shrugged his water canteen higher into his shoulder and moved carefully in the wake of Victoria's slow climb over the rocks. She was tiring fast, he thought; needed to rest up, get some proper sleep. But not yet. Nossir. She was still feisty and as determined as ever to get her hands on whatever she found in the caves.

But whom, when it came to it, would she really trust? Her years of hard-bitten life as a bar girl would have taught her some harsh lessons. She would know all about men when it came to the lure of gold, which meant she probably trusted nobody.

Even so, she was going to need *somebody* before she saw the Black Ridge Plain again.

And it was not going to be Frank Mattram, not if he had anything to do with it.

'Hey, Mattram,' called Bolteye, coming to a sweating halt, mopping feverishly at his brow. 'What say we rest up? Gettin' to be like a boiling pot out here. I'm for findin' some shade for a while. What yuh say, ma'am?'

Victoria merely wiped the sweat from her brow, and shrugged.

Mattram shielded his eyes for a moment against the glare of the peaks ahead, turned to stare at Victoria, then at Bolteye, and relaxed. 'Ten minutes. No more,' he announced. 'And I'm countin'. I wanna be at the caves up there by mid-afternoon.'

'Goin' to have to spend the night there, ain't we?' said Bolteye as they moved away to the shade of an overhang. 'We'll need best part of a day to shift what's stashed there – assumin', that is, we find the gold.' He grinned. 'And assumin', o'course, that our friend, Mr McKenna, ain't got some other notion in mind.'

'First sight I get of him, he's dead,' growled Mattram, turning angrily to stare into the peaks again.

Bolteye put a finger briefly to his lips as he caught Victoria's anxious glance and snapped the Winchester into a levelled aim. 'You ain't goin' to have that chance, Frank,' he drawled, steadying his balance and grip. 'I figure for you bein' all washed up here. You've done enough killin' even by my book. And that gold just ain't goin' to be for you. Not nohow.'

Mattram was a while before he shifted and turned to settle his gaze on Bolteye. 'My, my, ain't you somethin' nasty crawled out from under the stones?' he sneered, lounging his weight to one hip. 'You see this, lady? See what a snake we got for company?'

'You ain't in no position to talk like that, Mattram,' croaked Bolteye, prodding the rifle barrel into space. 'I got it settled in my mind what I gotta do, and I ain't for changin' it.'

'Always got to admire a man who sticks to his mind,' said Mattram almost nonchalantly. 'Shows he ain't for messin' with. What you reckon, ma'am?'

Victoria squirmed uncomfortably, then stiffened to her full height. 'You're mad, the pair of you,' she quipped, her eyes flashing. 'I would imagine you both have more than enough good reason for watching your backs without getting to fight each other.'

'Lady's talking some good sense there,' grinned Mattram.

'Don't change nothin',' croaked Bolteye. 'I seen what

I've seen with my own eyes, and I lost a good partner in these godforsaken rocks. I ain't for gamblin' no further.' He levelled the rifle again. 'Your time's up, Mattram.'

'That so?' said the gunslinger, shifting his weight to the other hip, hooking his thumbs in his belt. 'Do you really figure for me not reckonin' on a situation like this? That what you think – that I'd give a two-bits mountain drifter like you the time and space for stickin' a barrel in my gut? That I hadn't reckoned on your greed for the gold up there gettin' to you?' He gestured with one hand. 'Give me some credit, you old fool. I ain't that dim.' Mattram's stare blackened. 'Try pullin' the trigger on that piece.'

Bolteye's fingers fumbled at the trigger, twisted among themselves, worked feverishly for a moment, fell still as the man raised his pitiful gaze to Mattram's stare.

Victoria shuddered and hugged herself. Bolteye swallowed, the Winchester suddenly loose in his hands, the sweat glistening like ice on his brow.

'Well, now, ain't that just somethin'?' leered Mattram, drawing his Colt from its holster.

'How come—' began Bolteye.

'When you were sleepin',' said Mattram, spinning the Colt in his fingers. 'Didn't think I was goin' to let you near a hoard of stolen gold with a dangerous weapon like that in your hands, did you?'

Bolteye gulped again, blinked rapidly and let the rifle clatter uselessly into the rocks. Victoria made to move only to have her way barred as Mattram sprang forward with a growl, whipping the Colt across

Bolteye's cheek. Blood flowed freely. Victoria fell back. Mattram rushed on as Bolteye shrank to his knees, his arms whirling above his head to fend off the blows.

'Sonofa-goddamn-bitch,' cursed Mattram, raising the weapon for another lashing blow.

'Enough!' shrieked Victoria. 'Stop it! Stop it now!'

She pushed Mattram aside, leaving Bolteye the space and time to scramble out of reach.

'That's it – no more,' ordered Victoria, standing between the two men. 'You want to go ahead and kill each other, that's fine by me, but you're going to have to finish me first.' She glared, first at Mattram, then at Bolteye. 'You have a simple choice: we either go on together and reach the caves, or you two fight it out and none of us goes anywhere.'

'You win, lady,' wheezed Mattram, holstering the Colt. 'And you, mister, stay clear!'

Bolteye scowled as he wiped the blood from his face. 'And you, damn you . . .' he spluttered, 'you just watch your back!' He spat a tooth in a fount of thick spittle.

Victoria pulled and smoothed her clothes into place, swished her hair and flounced from the shade to the glare. 'Do as you both damn well please, I'm heading for gold!'

The men could only stare in silence.

McKenna smiled quietly, softly to himself as he watched Victoria moving confidently through the rocks ahead of the two men. She was looking purposeful, as if she had taken charge, at least for the moment; working her way easily over the rough going, the steps assured, the balance steady.

Mattram and the drifter, on the other hand, were almost contrite, stumbling in the woman's wake like reluctant mountain mules. Mattram had a darkness about him that suggested a suppressed anger that might boil over at any minute. The drifter was nursing some sort of wound, a bloody face that had not come about accidentally.

A falling out, pondered McKenna, shifting his body a fraction where he sprawled on the lip of a high shaded ledge? This soon, before they had come anywhere near the gleam of gold?

It figured, he thought. For Mattram, there was too much at stake for anyone to put so much as a finger out of place to disturb his plans. The mountain drifter had simply struck it lucky and was not for losing out without a fight.

But what of the woman, frowned McKenna, shifting again? She looked determined, as intent as ever on reaching the caves. And whatever her reasons, she was not about to be persuaded from them, not judging by the way she was still striding out there, refusing to look back, treating Mattram and the drifter as if they did not exist.

But what would she make of the bones when she reached them?

'You ain't goin' to hold to this pace for long, ma'am,' called Bolteye to Victoria's back. 'You should slow it some, take it easier. We're goin' to need all the strength we can raise for them caves up there.' He swung his lathered gaze to Mattram. 'What you say? Right, ain't I?'

'Why don't you shut it!' growled Mattram, stumbling at his side. 'Save your breath. I'll take care of the woman when the time comes.'

'Like you're goin' to take care of me *when the time comes*,' mocked Bolteye. 'The same go for McKenna? You included him in your plans? You figurin' on walkin' out of these mountains with all that gold for yourself, 'cus if you are—'

'You ain't one to be crowin' on that count. Not an hour back since you were plannin' on fillin' my gut full of lead!' Mattram swayed to hold his balance. 'More like you're the one figurin' on walkin' out a rich man.'

Bolteye dabbed a stained rag at his cheek. 'We go on like this, trustin' nobody, there ain't goin' to be any one of us leavin' the Scatterings alive, and that gold ain't goin' to be worth a spit.' He cursed as he cracked his shin. 'Why don't we—'

'Hold it,' clipped Mattram, shielding his gaze against the glare. 'What in the name of hell's fire has she found?'

The two men approached slowly, silently to where Victoria had halted, her gaze fixed wide-eyed on the skull perched on the rock slab.

Bolteye gulped and dabbed at a mixture of sweat and dried blood.

Mattram moved closer to the skull. 'Ben Foster,' he murmured through a dry, cracked breath. 'That's him right enough. Gotta be. Ben Foster. The one who never came back.'

TWENTY-ONE

'So just who was Ben Foster?' croaked Bolteye, still dabbing at the blood and sweat. 'Where'd he figure in all this?'

'He was the sixth member of the gang that made the raid at North Canyon: the three Pendrick brothers; Sloane, Cutchean and Foster,' said Mattram, squatting to examine the skeleton. 'After the raid, the gang headed for the foothills of the Scatterings and then split up. Charlie and his younger brother, Sam, headed south; Jack Cutchean rode east, Kid Sloane to the west. It was agreed that Fred Pendrick and Ben Foster would bury the gold somewhere in the mountains. The gang would come together for the share-out once the heat was off.'

Mattram came upright and returned to the skull. 'Only Fred came out of the mountains,' he murmured. 'He made the map and gave it to Charlie. Then the hand of fate got to work....'

Victoria staggered into the leanest shade, her expression empty, her face pale and drawn as Mattram continued:

'Sam Pendrick got himself killed in a drunken brawl; Fred took to the bottle and died in a roomin' house at Long Forks; Kid Sloane teamed up for a while with the Cutler boys and was shot in a bank raid out Oregon way. Only Charlie Pendrick and Jack Cutchean survived, and they. . . . Yeah, well, they're also history.'

Bolteye swallowed, blinked and sweated. 'And this heap of old bones is all that's left of Ben Foster. . . .'

'My father,' said Victoria from the shade.

The two men turned slowly to face her. 'Your pa?' mouthed Bolteye, his stare suddenly unblinking. 'You are. . . ?'

'Victoria Foster, only child of Ben and Martha Foster. My mother died soon after she realized pa was not coming home again, and I . . . I survived best I could, the only way open to me.' Victoria brushed a hot tear from her cheek. 'Then Charlie Pendrick came on the scene. He had no idea who I really was, but I knew of him well enough. Oh, yes. . . . And when he finally got to showing me the map, giving it to me for safe-keeping, setting off on this trek into the mountains, there was no doubt in my mind what I had to do.'

'You bet there wasn't!' scoffed Mattram. 'You're no better than us, lady. You want your hands on that gold as bad as we do, 'ceptin' for different reasons. But it don't change nothin', does it? That gold up there is still stolen, and your pa helped steal it!'

'Steady there,' urged Bolteye. 'The lady's just come face-on to the remains of her pa. Damnit, he's starin' at her even now! Ain't you got no respect?'

'All right,' snapped Mattram, his clenched teeth gleaming, 'so we've found Ben Foster and we'll cover his bones decent, but then that's it, we ain't wastin' no more time.' He pulled the map from his pocket, unfolded it and traced the marked spot with a finger as he scanned the line of caves above him. 'I reckon I got it figured,' he muttered. 'One more climb, and we'll be there. We'll see that gold before nightfall!' He folded the map and returned it to his pocket. 'Let's do what's necessary here and get movin'.'

Victoria shuddered, bit on her lip and stepped from the shade.

Bolteye tightened his gaze on the way ahead, noting for the second time since they had reached the bones the thin line of dirt and dust trickling from the high ledges. McKenna was up there, he thought, giving his cheek a final dab; there and watching every move they made.

But had he found the gold yet?

McKenna had watched intently as Mattram, the drifter and Victoria replaced the skull at the head of the bones and covered them with rocks and stones. Why all the concern, he had wondered? What was so special about this particular skeleton? Unless, of course, one of the three had been able to recognize the bones.

No time to debate the issue, he had decided, slipping away from the ledge to the tight, narrow track leading to the first of the caves.

If the remoteness of Bonnet Peak did in fact contain a 'hundred' caves among its maze of crags and reaches, he was not for counting them, thought McKenna, climbing steadily higher through the blaze of the burning sun. He would trust to his early reckoning: that by the time the raiders had carted their hoard this far, they would opt for hiding it in the first deep cave they discovered.

One of them would have stayed with the gold while

the other went ahead to seek out a suitable cave. He might have made this same climb, pondered McKenna; it was a near certainty he had suffered the same heat! But once he had reached the high ledge, which way then: to the left, to the right? The map had seemed to indicate the raider had chosen to go to the left.

McKenna halted, the sweat oozing freely into his shirt, blurring his vision for a moment before he cleared it with a wipe of his hand and a tight blink. He scanned the ledge track and caves to his right. Too narrow and too eaten away by wind and the seasonal winter rains for safety, he reckoned, turning his gaze to the left.

Here, as he had half expected, the ledge was a mite wider, firmer, protected from the full force of the whittling winds by the bulges of the main rock face. He grunted his satisfaction, clawed his way to the ledge and eased away to the left.

The first caves he reached warranted no more than a quick glance; too small, too shallow, he decided. The third was deeper and darker, but still not what a man with a fortune to hide would be looking for.

He moved on to a fourth cave, a fifth, the sixth, and was almost for turning back when he reached the seventh, paused at its mouth and peered into the thick, heavy gloom of the faintly musty interior. Something scuttled at his feet. He tensed, peered again, probing the depths for the slightest bulk of a shape that might mean. . . .

And then he saw it and the sweat ran cold.

'Goddamnit, you can almost taste it!' grinned Bolteye, slapping his lips and sniffing as if about to begin a hearty meal. 'They do say as how the old-time panners could smell gold long before they ever saw it. Reckon they were right at that. But me, I can taste it. Yessir! What you reckon, ma'am?'

Victoria wiped the dust and sticky smudges from her face. 'All I can taste is dirt!' she spat, blinking on the glare.

'Almost there,' choked Mattram, balancing himself on the scrambled rocks, his gaze penetrating the shimmer of heat to the rock face. 'Few more minutes and we can begin the climb. Once on to that ledge—'

'You spotted McKenna yet?' grunted Bolteye.

'Nothin',' said Mattram, his expression darkening again.

'Which means he's well ahead of us.' Bolteye fingered his swollen cheek. 'What you goin' to do if he's already in one of them caves? Supposin' he's found the gold. What then?'

'Ain't you overlookin' somethin'?' said Mattram.

'Tell me,' winced Bolteye.

'The lady here. Miss Foster,' grinned Mattram. 'My bettin' is McKenna ain't goin' to lift a finger if he figures the lady's in any sorta danger. Ain't that so, lady?'

'I wouldn't bet on it,' said Victoria. 'I wouldn't bet on anything that fella might or might not do. You've seen for yourself.'

'He know who you really are?' asked Bolteye.

'He knows,' said Victoria.

Mattram scraped his boot over a rock surface. 'About your pa? Who he was?'

'No, not about him. Only Pendrick. I told him about that sonofabitch.'

'Mebbe he's figurin' on takin' a share of the gold for

himself,' croaked Bolteye. 'Hell, he's only human like the rest of us, ain't he? Don't tell me he ain't been touched by the thought of gettin' rich.'

'I wouldn't bet on that either,' returned Victoria sharply. 'I think you might find McKenna's all for reporting this to the law in Dalton.'

'Over my dead body!' groaned Bolteye.

'Probably,' said Mattram. His gaze swung to Victoria. 'What about you? What are you plannin'? You've found the remains of your pa, you know what happened out here. And now you're within a spit of that hoard of gold. So what's you're thinkin'? What do you really want out of this?'

'She ain't no different,' snorted Bolteye. 'Gotta be smilin', ain't she? Hell, hoard like we got up there could set anybody up for life. No more smoky bars, eh, lady? No more two-bits trail-winders pawin' you; no more drunks, layabouts, gun-happy kids – you bet. That the situation? Don't tell me it ain't. You'd be lyin'.'

'Goin' to be enough to go round, ain't there?' said Mattram. 'Mebbe we could come to some sort of arrangement here. What say we split three ways? Each takes his share and rides on, goes his own way. Heck, we all of us got somethin' we want somewhere.'

'Ain't you the one overlookin' somethin' this time?' quipped Bolteye. 'Ain't you forgettin' our friend up there? I figure for McKenna havin' his own ideas.'

'That sonofabitch ain't goin'. . . .'

But Mattram's words were lost in the sudden shattering roar, whine and echo of a shot fired high above their heads.

A buzzard screamed its anger. Mattram swung his

Winchester into space. Bolteye pushed Victoria to the rocks and sank to her side on one knee. Three sets of eyes scanned and probed the higher reaches of the caves.

'You hearin' me loud and clear down there?' called McKenna, his voice echoing through the rocks.

'We hear you,' shouted Mattram. 'But don't you go reckonin'—'

'Just still that tongue of yours, Mattram, and listen up,' called McKenna again. 'And don't go figurin' on this bein' some showdown. It ain't. At the same time, don't get to makin' smart moves. I could down you faster than you could lift a finger.'

Mattram scowled and spat. Bolteye stroked his blood-streaked cheek and sweated. Victoria scanned the caves intently for the remotest hint of McKenna.

'I found the gold,' he announced, the echo spiralling across the heat haze. 'It's here, just like the map showed.'

Mattram grunted. Bolteye swallowed noisily.

'So what you plannin', mister?' shouted Mattram. 'You want we should come up there and help you shift it?'

'Precisely that. You leave your weapons with the lady and you, Mattram, along of that mountain man, climb up here, one ahead of the other. You do precisely as I tell you. One move out of place, and you're dead. No messin'. We do things my way. There ain't no other, and there sure as hell ain't the room up here for arguin' about it.' He paused. The echo faded. 'You followin' me?' he continued. 'You got it clear, or do I pick you off one at a time? Choice is yours.'

'You got it,' yelled Mattram, dropping his rifle to the rocks. 'We're comin' up.'

TWENTY-TWO

'We doin' the right thing here?' spluttered Bolteye, struggling through the rocks behind Mattram. 'You trust that fella? Hell, supposin' all we're doin' is providin' him with labour? Supposin' he shoots the pair of us minute we're all through with the haulin'?'

'You think I ain't thought of that?' Mattram was sweating, reaching for his next hold.

'Well, have you?' croaked Bolteye.

'We go along with McKenna, don't we? How else we goin' to get our hands on the gold? He's holdin' all the cards up there. Could take us out easy as spittin'. So we do as he says: leave our guns with the good lady and get to some honest toil for a while. Once we got the hoard on open ground—'

'And you figure he ain't thought of that?' moaned Bolteye.

'Sure he has. McKenna ain't no dumb dog. But on open ground, it's goin' to be two against one, ain't it? Me and you facin' him, and I'd fancy for us comin' out on top in a situation like that.'

'And the woman back there – what about her?' asked

Bolteye. 'Which side of the fence is she favourin'?'

'Said it yourself, didn't you?' grinned Mattram. 'She'll opt for anythin' that keeps her free of smoky bars and pawin' trail-hounds. You'll see. I ain't for mistakin' her type. They're all the same when you button it down.'

'Well,' muttered Bolteye, pausing to mop his face, 'I just hope you're right. Gold does strange things to folk. Twists them out of themselves. Shows up the other side. You don't take nothin' and nobody for granted where gold's concerned.' He eyed Mattram carefully. 'And that goes for everybody.'

'So I'd best watch my back, eh? That what you're tellin' me?'

Bolteye growled, grunted, spat, and clawed his way forward.

Victoria eased deeper into the scant cover, her boot brushing against the barrel of one of the discarded weapons. She could have picked up the rifle, taken it into her grip, levelled it against either of the two men struggling through the rocks to join McKenna at the mountain cave. She could have shot Mattram easily, without flinching, without feeling, knowing that he had been working with Charlie Pendrick and Jack Cutchean and was ready enough to double-cross even them, his so-called 'partners', when it came to the lure of gold. And as for Bolteye – he still wanted only one thing once he knew the gold was safe.

She shivered in spite of the glaring sun and haze of shimmering heat. She would do nothing, she decided. Not yet. Not here. Not with her mind still spinning with the images of the skeleton, the skull and now the vague memories from way back of her pa, of him leaving the ramshackle homestead out there on the panhandle, the look on her mother's face at the cold emptiness of the space he left behind. A space that was never filled.

She shivered again, blinked, swept a hand across her hot, sticky face and fixed her gaze on the progress of Mattram and Bolteye. Then smiled quietly, softly to herself as McKenna stepped into view from the caves, a rifle crooked almost nonchalantly in his arms.

Mattram reached the ledge, scanned the caves in a single glance, wiped the sweat from his face and stared at McKenna. 'Should've done somethin' about you hours back,' he croaked.

'Your mistake,' grinned McKenna, nursing the rifle to him. He watched in silence as Bolteye wheezed his bulk through the last of the climb and sweated to a halt. 'Right,' said McKenna, swinging the rifle to his shoulder, 'we got work to do.'

'Hold it there,' grunted Mattram, his stare sharpening. 'We've got a few things to get straight first.'

'Make it quick,' clipped McKenna. 'We've gotta be all through up here before dark.'

'What I want to know—' began Bolteye, only to be silenced by Mattram's raised arm and snap of his voice.

'How much gold you found back there?'

'Figured that might be your first consideration,' smiled McKenna. He relaxed his stance. 'Fifteen bags,' he said flatly.

Bolteye whistled through his broken teeth.

Mattram continued to stare. 'Fifteen,' he repeated softly, as if already calculating a share-out.

'That is some hoard,' hissed Bolteye, dabbing absently at his swollen cheek. 'Some hoard . . . enough to keep a fella in style and luxury all his days. Why, with wealth like that—'

'So what's your plan, McKenna?' clipped Mattram again, his stare still sharp and unblinking.

'We shift it,' said McKenna. 'Simple as that. What *I* decide to do with it once it's out of the cave—'

'What *you* decide?' spluttered Bolteye. 'Now you ease up there, fella. Me and Mattram and the lady there might have a whole heap of other ideas on that score. Sure, we'll help you shift the gold, but once we got it back to them mules of mine, well, we're sure as hell goin' to have some discussin' to do.'

'No discussions,' snapped McKenna. 'You don't like it, I can put you out of your misery right now.'

Bolteye gulped and went back to dabbing his cheek. Mattram's stare softened instantly as he shrugged and eased the sticky bite of his hat. 'You're dealin', mister,' he said quietly. 'We go along with what you say.' He turned his head to look back to the sprawl of rocks and boulders and the lean shade where Victoria waited and watched. ' 'Course, can't speak for the lady down there. She's had a nasty shock, comin' across them bones like she did.' He glanced at McKenna. 'You wouldn't know, but that skeleton is all that's left of her pa.' Mattram waited a moment. 'He was one of Pendrick's gang. Somebody decided he was not for bein' counted in the share-out.'

'That somebody bein' Fred Pendrick,' spat Bolteye. 'He was the one who took out the woman's pa, Ben Foster.' He spat again. 'That's what gold does for a fella. I seen it before.'

'Yeah, well, that's as maybe,' said Mattram. 'Point I'm makin' is, we should be figurin' for the lady havin' her own thoughts on what happens to the gold. Kinda got a blood interest in it, ain't she? What you reckon, McKenna?'

McKenna was staring at her, long and hard, in the same way he had on that wind-whipped day out there on the plain. Victoria shielded her eyes as the light dazzled through the rocks. Why was he staring so intently? What had Mattram and Bolteye said. . . . She swallowed drily. The bones; the skeleton. They would have told McKenna that the remains were those of her pa. He would be piecing together the whole sorry story. She wiped a tear from her cheek and backed deeper into the shade.

It was some minutes before McKenna finally turned away, his rifle still shouldered, to direct Mattram and Bolteye to the dark mouth of one of the larger caves.

Victoria watched, her gaze tight and straining against the glare for every movement as the shadowy shapes of the three men blurred on the darkness of the cave and disappeared. She swallowed again, fidgeted with the collar of her shirt, wiped the sweat from her neck, concentrated, sighed, began for a moment to panic, to wish that she had never seen the Scatterings and let McKenna do as he had wanted and take her to Dalton.

Too late now. She was here, had found the grisly

evidence of her pa's part in the North Canyon bank raid; men had died for the map, and the promise of gold was still the deadly lure it had always been.

She took a step forward as Mattram and Bolteye came back to the light and the ledge, each carrying a small bag.

A sudden chill squirmed through her sweat.

'How long we goin' to keep this up?' hissed Bolteye into Mattram's ear as they eased the bags to the ground. 'We ain't goin' to dance to his tune, are we? He's mebbe plannin' on handin' this lot back to the bank, f'cris'sake!'

'Mebbe he is,' muttered Mattram. 'I don't give a damn – but this ain't the time to make a move. I'll tell you when. Meantime—'

'Let's keep it movin' here,' ordered McKenna from the mouth of the cave. 'Another couple of hours and the light'll be fadin'.'

'And I ain't for bein' up here come nightfall,' grinned Bolteye, rubbing his hands together. 'We'll be through long before that.' He ducked as he moved into the cave's cooler gloom. 'How much do you figure for bein' stashed here?'

'I ain't countin',' said McKenna. 'And neither are you. There ain't the time. Just shift it.'

'Tell me somethin', McKenna.' Mattram frowned, coming to his side, 'what did you feel when you scrambled into this hole and saw that hoard just piled there? You must've felt somethin'. Hell, t'ain't every day a fella has that sort of encounter. Not even a man of your experience.' His cynical grin hovered on the twitch of a nerve.

McKenna swung the rifle from his shoulder to cradle it in his arms. 'Remind me to tell you sometime.' He smiled briefly before his steady gaze darkened without blinking.

'I will,' said Mattram, turning to the hoard.

It took almost the full two hours to carry the bags from the cave, lower them to the flatter level and cart them on to the closest cover.

'Light's fadin' fast,' McKenna had eventually announced when the last bag had been moved. 'This is as far as we go for tonight. We rest up some and begin shiftin' the gold to the mules at dawn, soon as we're sure of our footin'.'

'And then?' said Mattram. 'Where do we go from there?'

'One thing at a time,' grunted McKenna.

'What do you reckon, ma'am?' asked Bolteye, wiping the dirt from his cheeks. 'You ain't had a deal to say over this, seein' as how it was you who had the map in the first place. Reckon you've got as big a share in this as anybody, specially after what you found here and you bein' Ben Foster's daughter. Gotta have feelin's, ain't you?'

'I have my feelings, make no mistake about that,' said Victoria sharply, her gaze moving coldly from Bolteye to Mattram, to the stacked bags of gold, and then to the crags and peaks. She shrugged. 'It seems to me the sooner we're out of these mountains the better.'

'Now there's the first sensible comment I've heard in days,' grinned Mattram. 'Let's do just that, shall we? Get the hell out of here, fast as we can. We could have this hoard shifted an hour after sun-up and the foothills to Black Ridge Plain in our sights by nightfall t'morrow. Be clear and away in a day and a half – two at most.'

McKenna coughed lightly and tapped the toe of his boot on a rock. 'And you, Mattram, in the hands of the law before the week's out.'

Mattram's hand fell instinctively to his empty holster. 'Two-bits to a spit, I'd take you out now, mister, if I had a piece.'

'Think I ain't aware of that?' grated McKenna. He stared hard and bleakly for a moment. 'Like I said, we rest up. We'll be movin' again before full light. We've got water and there's mebbe enough dry timber around to light a fire. And that's it. The weapons stay with me. You ain't got no need for 'em.' He paused as he shouldered the rifle. 'And just in case you get to wonderin', I'm stayin' with the gold.'

'Wait 'til it's full dark,' whispered Mattram from beneath the tipped brim of his hat where he lay with his back to a rock.

Bolteye, resting at his side, grunted a response and focused his gaze through the gathering gloom on McKenna and the woman. 'What they got to say between 'em that's so important?'

'Two guesses,' murmured Mattram.

'Figurin' when, where and how they're goin' to get rid of us, so's they can keep the gold for themselves.'

'Somethin' like that,' said Mattram. 'But not before they've used us to help shift the hoard to the mules, which is why, my friend, we gotta make a move before first light.'

'Take 'em out, the pair of 'em, or just McKenna?' croaked Bolteye. 'I ain't much for killin' the woman.'

'We save her for later. What we really need is a weapon. One of them Winchesters McKenna's guardin'. I'll take care of the rest.'

'What's that mean?' frowned Bolteye, running a hand over his face.

'Just what I'm sayin', you fool. We get a rifle. Get control of the situation. We ain't goin' to be spendin' a dollar of that gold 'til we've got our hands on it.'

Bolteye sniffed and squinted as the gloom thickened. 'How much do you figure on bein' there?'

'Enough,' said Mattram, his sidelong glance gleaming from beneath the hat-brim. 'More than enough.'

He smiled softly to himself.

TWENTY-THREE

Bolteye tensed, tight as a spooked rattler, his eyes wide and concentrated on McKenna. The fella was not for sleeping, not even dozing, simply resting, perched on a rock slab at the side of the gold. He was just sat there, relaxed, quiet as a mouse, his hands easy on the Winchester, his gaze soft on the night and its shapes, the high moon and stars. A man thinking his own thoughts, mused Bolteye.

Which meant his reactions might be just a touch slower.

'In your own time,' hissed Mattram without moving. 'But f'cris'sake make it sound convincing. McKenna ain't dumb.'

Bolteye swallowed as he switched his focus to the sleeping woman. 'What about her?' he murmured. 'She ain't no fool either.'

'Leave her to me. You just get on with what you got to do – and don't waste no more time.'

Bolteye swallowed again, wiped his face and came slowly, unsteadily to his feet, one hand clamped firmly across his gut as he groaned a slow path towards McKenna.

'Hey, fella,' he moaned, his eyes round and glassy, 'I got one helluva pain here. Mebbe some sorta rot in the water or somethin'. Need to get into them rocks there.' He retched, spat and groaned again.

'Make it quick and stay in sight,' said McKenna, standing upright.

'This is goin' to be kinda private if you don't mind,' croaked Bolteye.

'Just get on with it,' quipped McKenna, cradling the Winchester across his body.

Bolteye cringed away into the darkness among the deeper rocks.

'Far enough,' said McKenna, turning from the stacked gold to be certain he still had the moonlit bulk of Bolteye in his view. 'You ain't hackin' your way to no trail.'

Bolteye had halted, his mind spinning with the thought of what he should do next, his eyes wet with the effort of probing the night, when he heard the thud of the rock into McKenna's back, saw him stumble, lose his balance, the rifle clattering from him to the ground; he was already striding across the rocks as Mattram sprang from the darkness, another rock aimed for McKenna's head.

'Don't overdo the nursin'. He ain't worth it.' Mattram spat loudly and deliberately into the rocks, his gaze cold on Victoria's face. 'Just stop that bleedin' and get him back on his feet.' He glanced only briefly at the unconscious body of McKenna, the wound on the back of his head, the stained bandanna in Victoria's hand.

'He goin' to live?' asked Bolteye, hunching his shoulders against the night chill.

'Of course he's going to live,' flared Victoria, tending the wound. 'You don't kill this fellow that easy.'

Mattram spat again. 'Cut the mouthin', lady. We don't need it. All we need is to get movin', minute the light comes up.'

'This isn't going to work,' said Victoria. 'I hope you realize that.'

Mattram settled his grip on the Winchester in his arms, and smiled cynically. 'You figure, eh? Well, we ain't doin' so bad so far. I'm runnin' the show again, I've got the weapons, and McKenna ain't much use to anybody right now. I'd say things are workin' just fine.'

'*We*'re runnin' the show,' added Bolteye. 'Don't go forgettin' that.'

Mattram nodded and turned his attention to the darkness. 'Give it another hour and we can start movin',' he murmured. 'Get the gold to the mules and plan a way back to the plain.'

'And the waiting reception,' mocked Victoria with a toss of her head. 'You don't imagine the stageline won't be looking for you, do you? Not to mention the law. I wouldn't be at all surprised if the Black Ridge Plain isn't swarming with men. They might even be here, in the mountains.'

'She's mebbe got a point there,' said Bolteye. 'Hell . . . and me and poor old Mr Burns only got into this 'cus—'

' 'Cus yuh got greedy and blinded by the prospect of gold, and don't you say no other,' spat Mattram. 'Same goes for the whole bunch, 'specially the lady here.' His face beaded with an anxious sweat. 'Ain't that so, ma'am? Ain't you just as fevered at the thought of gettin' your hands on this hoard here? Sonofa-goddamn-bitch you are! Can see it in your eyes. And I'd reckon for you goin' just about as far as it takes to make sure you do.'

Victoria's stare was wide and flashing and her anger welling in her throat when McKenna stirred, groaned and opened his eyes.

They began at the first hint of light under Mattram's orders. 'We ain't goin' to make this any more difficult than necessary,' he said, the Winchester levelled in a steady grip on Victoria and McKenna. 'And we do the whole thing neat and tidy, no rushin', and no gettin' smart.' He eyed McKenna through a tight stare. 'You hear that, McKenna? No messin'. That lump on the back of your head don't fool me none. Teach you to be more careful next time. All right, then, let's move.'

It was not so much the rough going, the weight and bulk of the hoard that dictated their pace as the lack of any consistent strength of light. They were probing for a foothold through the straggling shadows of the last of night in one moment, blinking on the skittish first light in the next. Shapes and rock formations did not stay the same for more than minutes; crags appeared and disappeared in the sudden creep of dawn mist; boulders grew and faded; the track to the mules hitched on the lower reaches came and dropped away in an instant.

They had been moving close on a half-hour before

Victoria drew alongside McKenna. 'You going to make it?' she whispered. 'The bleeding's stopped, but the wound looks ugly.'

'Feels ugly,' murmured McKenna.

She had shuddered in spite of the effort and weight she was carrying. 'You had any thoughts—'

'Plenty,' said McKenna, 'but none of 'em makin' a deal of sense right now. Just watch Mattram for the rattler he is. He's goin' to have to make another move soon.'

'What sort of move?' Victoria frowned.

'Just keep watchin'.'

Another long, silent, mist-drenched hour and they had finally left the plateau, the bones of Ben Foster and the yawning mouths of the Hundred Caves and reached the mules and the track back to the foothills.

'So far, so good,' Mattram drawled, watching carefully as Bolteye stacked the hoard. 'Next, we get these mules watered, loaded up and ready to move. I ain't for spendin' any more time in these goddamn rocks.' He patted the butt of the Winchester. 'Gettin' to the end of things, ain't we?' He grinned. 'Only question now is, when and where we get to the share-out?'

'You bet!' beamed Bolteye. 'And I been thinkin' as how we should come to it real soon. I mean, there ain't nothin' to be had in waitin', is there? In any case, I got ideas on trekking out some ways deeper west, into the lower ranges, before I push on to mebbe Colorado territory. I got old partners out there. So I figure for takin' my share and a mule right now. Hell, I know these mountains well enough. Could be miles away and out of sight—'

'Well, now, I been reckonin' for you being *out of sight*, Mr Mountain Man,' smiled Mattram. 'Just that: way 'out of sight', if you get my meanin'.'

Bolteye's stare narrowed and darkened. 'And just what do you mean by that, mister? Or need I ask?'

Victoria tensed on a trickle of cold sweat down her spine. McKenna did not move.

'You see, we got a problem here,' said Mattram, his fingers drumming lightly on the rifle. 'We've got an awful lot of gold here. You might almost say too much. Hell, ain't that somethin' to ponder?' His smile widened for a moment, then faded on his grey expression. 'And with all that wealth available, we gotta be very careful about who gets to hearin' of it, ain't we? Very careful, I'd reckon. You ridin' off to Colorado territory, for instance. Why, there ain't no tellin' as to who might get to askin' questions, is there? Who's this mountain drifter with all this money, they might ask? Where'd he come by it? And before you know it you could be attractin' the attentions of all manner of hardbitten lawmen.'

Bolteye gritted his teeth, heaved on a deep breath and stared like a hawk into Mattram's face. 'You schemin' what I think you're schemin'? You bet, eh? Oh, yes, you bet to it! You're fixin' on my share findin' its way along of yours. 'Course you are.' His eyes flicked to Victoria. 'Then it'll be your turn, ma'am.' He spat to within a finger of Mattram's boot. 'That the way of it, Frank? That how it's goin' to be? I should've known. . . .'

Bolteye had half turned to the weapons ranged at the side of the bags of gold, bent to lay his hands on the nearest and was within a second of lifting it to his grip when Mattram's Winchester roared like something bursting from the darkest depths of the mountain.

Bolteye groaned, flung his arms above his head and crashed face down in the rocks.

Victoria gasped and shuddered.

McKenna had taken a step forward, but was halted where he stood as the Winchester swung round to level on him.

'You shot him in the back,' hissed Victoria, her eyes flashing on Mattram.

'In the back, in the head, who the hell cares?' sweated Mattram, levelling the rifle on McKenna again. 'And don't you get to no heroics, mister. I ain't in the mood.'

'So was he right – is this what you're planning?' snapped Victoria. 'You're taking the gold for yourself. All of it. You intended it all along.'

Mattram's stare burned, flared, subsided and settled as he relaxed, licked at the sweat on his lips, and smiled softly. 'You got it, lady, 'ceptin' for one thing: your own part in all this.'

Victoria stiffened and tossed her hair. 'My part?' she quipped. 'There's no part for me. Not here there isn't.'

'Wrong,' said Mattram, the smile twitching. 'So wrong. You think it through now. We've got the gold, the means of gettin' it out of these mountains, and once out there – clear of the rocks and across the plain headin' south for the border – there ain't nothin' can hold us.' His eyes came alight again. 'You could have anythin' you took a fancy to: a spread fit for a duchess; land, stock, clothes, jewels – there ain't nothin' you couldn't have. And me right along of you to make sure nobody takes it from you. What you say? We get rid of McKenna here and keep movin'? You with me, lady?'

Victoria stiffened again, adjusted the set of her shirt, hitched her pants, and glanced quickly at McKenna. 'Sure,' she grinned, 'and why not? What have we got to lose?'

'Now you're really talkin'!' beamed Mattram, the sweat glistening like a hoar-frost on his black stubble. 'Always figured for you comin' round to sensible thinkin'. Just knew you would. Seen it in your face when you were stringin' old Charlie Pendrick along back there. You ain't nobody's fool, lady, and that's for sure.'

Victoria stepped deliberately between Mattram and McKenna. 'Glad to hear you think so, Mr Mattram,' she acknowledged. 'But that don't mean I approve of shooting men in the back, whoever they might be. So there'll be no more of that. As for McKenna here . . .' she hesitated, her gaze shifting for a moment to the tip of her boot. 'As for him, I'll decide his fate.'

'Let me finish it here, ma'am,' protested Mattram. 'Get it over with. Hell, what's the difference, anyhow? Here, out there, I don't see as how—'

'I'll decide,' snapped Victoria. 'No more to be said on the matter.' She tossed her hair again. 'Now let's get that body out of the reach of buzzards and the gold loaded. We have a long way still to go.' She swung round to face McKenna. 'I'm sure our good friend here will be more than happy to help.'

McKenna stayed silent, but his long stare was unblinking as it fixed Victoria then moved slowly to where Mattram was already shifting the first of the sacks to the mules.

Victoria frowned and flicked her eyes to her left to the track that wound back to a smothering sprawl of boulders.

'I figure for us headin' due south-east once we hit the plain,' said Mattram, his back to Victoria. 'There's a homestead over Four Breaks where I got a long-time partner who still owes me. We'll buy ourselves a couple of horses there.'

'Sure,' answered Victoria, drawing McKenna's attention to her again while Mattram worked on. 'Sounds good.' She flicked her eyes back to the track and mouthed silently.

'You bet to it,' Mattram went on. 'I thought all this through. I ain't spittin' on no sneaky wind when it comes to gold. But it takes a whole lot more. . . .'

It was the scrambling of McKenna's boots over stones and rocks, the gasp and groan from Victoria, that swung Mattram round from the gold, sent his fingers clawing instinctively for his Winchester, swinging it to his grip and blazing wildly at the disappearing shape of McKenna.

'What the hell!' cursed Mattram, pushing Victoria aside as he lunged towards the boulders. 'What you let him do that for? Should've shot the sonofabitch right there, damn it. Where'd he go?' His eyes narrowed in a haze of sweat and anger.

Victoria bit on her grin and wiped the sudden swirl of dirt from her face.

TWENTY-FOUR

'Stay here. Watch the mules – and the gold. And don't move, you hear?' Mattram ran a smeared, wet hand over his lips and glared at Victoria through bloodshot eyes. 'I'll go get McKenna. And this time I'll finish it, good and proper, for all time.' He spat, stroked the barrel of the rifle and turned his glare on the mound of boulders and the rocks and crags beyond them. 'The rat ain't armed, so this shouldn't take long. I wanna be movin' before. . . .'

He stepped back hurriedly, pushing Victoria into a shadowed cleft at a dust-swirling fall of rock to his right. He coughed, wiped his eyes and narrowed his gaze on the higher reaches. 'Sonofabitch,' he mouthed on a spitting hiss. 'He's up there, damn him.' He offered a hand to Victoria. 'You all right? Just keep clear. Get with the mules back there.'

Victoria eased away. 'McKenna's no stranger to these mountains,' she murmured. 'He won't give up without a fight.'

'So whose side you on?' sneered Mattram. 'He might know these goddamn rocks, but he don't know the real

Frank Mattram. Not yet he don't. But he will!'

He slapped the rifle, flashed a leering grin at Victoria and climbed into the boulders.

He was out of Victoria's sight within seconds, a scrambling shape reaching for handholds. And then nothing save the sound of boots on rock, the occasional grunt, a hissed curse until she finally stared in silence, the light beginning to burn in its strengthening brightness.

She moved quickly to the weapons stacked with the gold, picked up a Winchester and stumbled her way into the clefts at the foot of the boulders. She would follow in Mattram's steps, somehow get the rifle to McKenna. A crazy scheme perhaps, but, damn it, it was the best they had right now.

A trickling line of loose dirt to her left halted her for a moment. She waited, swallowing, licking at salty sweat, listening for another movement. Nothing. She blinked and moved on, climbing confidently now, feeling for the holds without wondering if they would support her weight, crack or splinter.

More dirt, tumbling stones, a cloud of dust almost blinding her. And then the crack of Mattram's voice.

'McKenna? You hearin' me up there? You sure had better be. Good and clear.'

Victoria halted again. She heard the man spit, curse as he reached for a firmer hold.

'I'm goin' to say this only once,' he croaked on, gathering his breath in deep gulps. 'There ain't the time for more discussion and debatin'. You had your chance way back, and now you're on your own. Pity. You could have been a wealthy man. Now the only prospect you got is bein' a dead one.' He spat again. 'Five minutes – that's all it's goin' to take for me to get to where you are. Five minutes. And I'm countin'. . . .'

Victoria gasped, swallowed a groan and blinked on another swirl of dust. The sweat ran like tears down her cheeks as she scanned and peered frantically for some sight of McKenna.

Damn it, where was he holed up? How high into the rocks had he climbed? He must have heard Mattram's threats, perhaps even seen him, but offered no response. Was he hiding, waiting? He might even try making a run for it, getting clear while he still had a chance.

No time now to continue climbing in Mattram's steps, Victoria decided, he would outpace her in minutes. She had to find another way, climb out of Mattram's reach.

She glanced quickly left to right. No choice. She had to go to the right.

The gap between the two vast boulders was narrow, a tight fit for even her trim figure, but she made it and stumbled breathless and sweat-soaked into a more open area that sloped to what seemed from where she stood to be a smaller, levelled space.

She stumbled on.

'You countin' down the time, McKenna?' called Mattram again, his voice echoing through the rocks. 'I sure as hell am, and by my reckonin'. . . .'

The first boulder crashed from the higher rocks with a rumbling roar that grew like thunder. A second followed quickly in its wake. Victoria watched wide-eyed as a cloud of dust lifted, thickened and swirled, then massed as if in flood to pour through the boulders in a tumbling grey tide.

There were moments of silence before Mattram's voice rose again.

'Nice try, McKenna,' he choked, 'but I was figurin' you might resort to stone-throwin'. Better luck next time – if there is a next time!' He laughed and spat. 'I'm still countin'!'

Victoria cursed quietly to herself, wiped the dust from her face and lips and scrambled on to the slope, trying now to fathom just where McKenna had been when he launched the boulders. Hard to say, she reckoned, but Mattram had to be closing. Surely it was only a matter of time before he had McKenna in his sights.

Sooner than she thought.

The single shot cracked, echoed, then faded on Mattram's cackling laughter. 'Gettin' closer, McKenna. You bet on it! Next time I squeeze on this trigger could be the last time.'

Victoria had reached the top of the slope, halted, gasping for breath on the effort, the heat and the still drifting dust-cloud. She cursed again, wiped her neck and had figured on crossing to the far side of the levelled space when McKenna launched himself like a hawk from a ledge above her, fell silently through the dust-smudged light and thudded to the ground only yards from where she stood.

'Thanks,' he wheezed, a hand already outstretched for the Winchester. 'Reckoned for you makin' it. But there ain't much time. In fact. . . .'

Another shot blazed, echoed, spinning McKenna round to face the crouched, advancing shape of

Mattram, the Winchester levelled in his grip, a grin cracking the sweat-caked dirt at his lips, his eyes gleaming like polished stones.

'Knew it. Just knew it,' he scowled, releasing a spitting blaze from the rifle that threw Victoria off her feet, blood oozing freely through her shirt above her breast.

The last she heard before the light and the day faded was the unrelenting roar of a Winchester shattering the high mountain silence.

'She's awake and waitin' on you,' said the doctor, closing the door to the room as McKenna approached down the corridor.

'How's she doin'?' asked McKenna, removing his hat.

'Well on the way to bein' what I imagine is her usual feisty self. A whole sight brighter-eyed than when you brought her in three days back.'

The doctor adjusted the set of the collar to his frockcoat and peered carefully over the rims of his spectacles. 'Some escapade you had out there by all accounts. Sheriff Rhodes has been tellin' me all about it. You were lucky, the pair of you. If Dalton had been another five miles down the trail, them mules – never mind the woman there – would never have made it.' He grunted knowledgeably. 'Touch and go, mister, touch and go. Lady had lost a lot of blood. But—' he shrugged his shoulders – 'she's made it. And you did the right thing bringin' her in as fast as you did. Give it a week and she'll be fine.'

'Grateful for what you've done,' said McKenna, turning his hat through his hands.

'A word of advice, however.' The doctor peered more intently. 'I ain't under no illusions as to the nature of her past life and the occupation she's been followin'. See it a dozen times a week in my profession. But I'd reckon for them days bein' over. For ever.' He grunted again as he glanced quickly over the dimly lit walls of the corridor. 'A month ago she'd have been perfectly at home in a place like this. The Split Dollar saloon in Dalton ain't no different from a hundred others. But not, I suspect, the sort of place for Miss Foster any longer. So, if you do happen to have a say in the shapin' up of her future, mister, I'd figure for you gettin' her out of town and headin' some place where there's mebbe good clean air soon as you can.'

'Well, I hadn't reckoned—' croaked McKenna.

'She's all yours,' announced the doctor, donning his hat dramatically. 'I bid you good day. I'll look in on the lady later.'

McKenna hesitated a moment, watched the man disappear down the stairs to the bar, then tapped lightly on the door and opened it at Victoria's bidding.

'Good to see you.' She smiled from the bed where she lay propped on a wave of pillows. 'I was wondering when it might be, but I guess you've had things to do.' She gestured to the chair at the side of the bed. 'Please sit down.'

McKenna nodded as he sat uncomfortably, turning his hat in his hands.

'Gotta say you're lookin' a whole heap better, ma'am,' he said nervously. 'Had my real doubts back there . . . meanin', o'course—'

'I know exactly what you mean, Mr McKenna. Fact

is I owe my life to you. Saying thank you hardly seems enough, but I do, anyhow.'

They waited in a thin silence for a moment.

'I was going to say—' began Victoria.

'Like you say ma'am, I been busy since we hit town,' quipped McKenna hurriedly, on a deeper breath. 'Sheriff here had raised a posse when the stage didn't turn up, but they found nothin' and trailed nowhere. Winds had buried the tracks. He was all set for startin' again when we turned up.' He paused, staring at his hat. 'I told him the full story, ma'am. Everythin'. He knows all about you – leastways, much as I know myself – and knew plenty about Mattram. He recalled the raid at North Canyon well enough, but had no notion, o' course, of what had finally panned out between the robbers.'

'What about the gold, Mr McKenna?' said Victoria sharply. 'What happened to it? What did you do?'

'I left it ma'am, right where it was. Right there in the mountains.'

Victoria was silent for a moment. 'You left it,' she murmured at last. 'Just that? Left it.'

'Yes, ma'am, didn't have no choice as I saw it. It was you or the gold. Couldn't handle both with only two mules.' He came to his feet and walked to the window overlooking the street, conscious of Victoria's eyes following him. 'Mattram was dead, but you, ma'am, were alive, though bleedin' bad.

'Anyhow, I managed to bandage you best I could, fix you on a mule and bring up the second for m'self and as a spare if need be. We trailed slow out of the Scatterings, me walkin' most of it, but you held up there and we finally made it to the plain. Wasn't too bad from there into Dalton, even though you were beginnin' to fade some by the time—'

'You left *all* the gold, Mr McKenna?' Victoria frowned. 'All the bags. Every last one?'

'Yes, ma'am,' said McKenna turning from the window. 'Didn't see no need for it. Figured for gettin' you to a doc to be the priority.'

Victoria stared at him without blinking, her expression suddenly bland and lost. 'You've told the sheriff?' she murmured again. 'You've explained all this – about the map, the gold, my father, what we found of him, where you left the hoard?'

'Oh, yes, ma'am, Sheriff Rhodes knows the full story. He's informed the bank at North Canyon and I'm told there'll be a posse leavin' here today to recover the gold.' He examined the brim of his hat. 'Sheriff says as how there won't be no charges against yourself and there'll likely as not be a handsome reward from the bank. He ain't sure how much.'

Victoria slumped into the pillows. 'It's yours, Mr McKenna. You've earned it.'

'No, ma'am, we'll share it. That's only fair. Half and half. Down the middle.'

Victoria sat upright again. 'And what will you do with your share?' she asked.

'Well, ma'am, I been thinkin' on that, and I figure there's only so much wealth a fella can handle and still be of a settled mind. So I reckon on headin' out of this territory, leavin' the Scatterings to themselves and their ghosts, and trailin' to the bluegrass country. Get myself some good clean air, open spaces and mebbe a small homestead. I figure that for bein' riches enough. And you, ma'am, what would you be plannin' on doin'. . . ?'

Victoria was still resting contentedly long after she was alone again in the room and the afternoon shadows had cooled the heat at the window. Bluegrass country, clean air, open spaces, a small homestead, McKenna close by, were prospects that grew brighter and more desirable by the hour. She smiled softly to herself. You might say they were almost golden in their promise.

LC